a certain october

ALSO BY ANGELA JOHNSON

a certain october

ANGELA JOHNSON

SIMON & SCHUSTER BFYR

New York   London   Toronto   Sydney   New Delhi

SIMON & SCHUSTER BFYR

An imprint of Simon & Schuster Children's Publishing Division
1230 Avenue of the Americas, New York, New York 10020

This book is a work of fiction. Any references to historical events, real people,
or real locales are used fictitiously. Other names, characters, places, and
incidents are products of the author's imagination, and any resemblance to
actual events or locales or persons, living or dead, is entirely coincidental.

For information about special discounts for bulk purchases,
please contact Simon & Schuster Special Sales at 1-866-506-1949 or
business@simonandschuster.com.
The Simon & Schuster Speakers Bureau can bring authors to your live event.
For more information or to book an event, contact
the Simon & Schuster Speakers Bureau at 1-866-248-3049 or visit our
website at www.simonspeakers.com.
Book design by Laurent Linn
The text for this book is set in Aldine.
Manufactured in the United States of America
2 4 6 8 10 9 7 5 3 1
Library of Congress Cataloging-in-Publication Data
Johnson, Angela, 1961–
A certain October / Angela Johnson. — 1st ed.
p. cm.

Summary: "Scotty compares herself to tofu: no flavor unless you add
something. And it's true that Scotty's friends, Misha and Falcone, and her
brother, Keone, make life delicious. But when a terrible accident occurs,
Scotty feels responsible for the loss of someone she hardly knew, and the
world goes wrong. She cannot tell what is a dream and what is real. Her
friends are having a hard time getting through to her and her family is
preoccupied with their own trauma. But the prospect of a boy, a dance, and
the possibility that everything can fall back into place soon help Scotty realize
that she is capable of adding her own flavor to life."—Provided by publisher.

ISBN 978-0-689-86505-3 (hardback)
[1. Death—Fiction. 2. Friendship—Fiction. 3. Autism—Fiction. 4. High
schools—Fiction.] I. Title.
PZ7.J629Cer 2012
[Fic]—dc23
2012001595
ISBN 978-1-4424-1726-7 (eBook)

FIRST
EDITION

For Alyssa

a certain october

PART 1

Sometimes Tofu Is Just Tofu

1

IN THE FUTURE, WHEN I IMAGINE I MIGHT BE famous or infamous for something I've done, I suppose people will ask what it was that brought me to that place. Well, if I'm infamous I will say—no eyewitnesses and a good lawyer. If I'm famous I will say, I guess I just wanted it bad enough. One of these scenarios will probably be true, but more than likely neither will happen.

Most likely I'll live my life like most people on the planet. Highs, lows, buy some shit, read some books, love some people, try not to eff the world up, and be kind to animals so they won't eat me, as I've chosen to try not to eat them.

But if I'm ever asked if there was a time in my life that made me the person I am, I will point to a certain October that stays with me like a song played over the radio a hundred times at the start of a day. You can't get it out of your head so all you can do is go through it. I never did finish my book report on *Anna Karenina* and I went through so much with people I loved and hung out with. I got to see the world through their eyes that certain October, although my own were slightly unfocused.

First I hear,

"Where are the damned cookies?"

Then.

"Where the hell are the damned cookies?"

Then, "Paul, did you do something the hell with the damned cookies?"

Then, "Scotty—get down here."

I stumble down the steps from my warm, train-wreck, and totally needing a makeover bedroom, walking over picture books about trains and planes and automobiles; then I walk over more picture books about planes and trains and automobiles in the living room. By the time I trip out of the living room and walk down the hall towards the kitchen, I've passed more bookshelves filled with books about trains and planes. They are all my brother Keone's.

My father is always chilled and never raises his voice. My grandmama says that they always worried about him getting run over by people 'cause he was so laid-back. Not to diss my grandmama or anything, but you don't have to scream louder than anybody in the room to get your way and shut people up.

So Daddy, at the kitchen table, whispers—"Laura, why are you screaming about cookies at eight o'clock in the morning? Why are the cookies damned and why would you think I'd involve hell in my plot to keep them from you?"

Damn!

My dad's a mediator with the union.

Laura looks at me sucking down my first cup of coffee and shakes her head because Dad hasn't taken his eyes off of what he's reading. That's a mad skill in my book. One day I hope to answer Mr. Permowitz's algebra questions while I calmly read about where all the movie stars are going for summer vacation while drawing french fries around the ones who might soon need an underweight intervention.

Something doesn't feel right around the kitchen—you know, besides the fact of Laura's

ANGELA JOHNSON

cookie obsession. I love Laura. She's funny and she doesn't take shit from anybody. And she'll go to the end to help you. Mostly, though, she gets a little too pumped up about things. Now that I've put some caff in my blood I'm feeling friendlier and decide to ask about the cookie thing when out of nowhere my wet naked seven-year-old brother Keone shoots out of the pantry past us in the kitchen, flies out the door, and makes a Usain Bolt sprint for the street.

We all start running.

We don't find him in the front yard or the street. We look for him in the garage and behind the garage. We look to see if he's hiding behind the dead ten feet of garden sunflowers back by the fence. We even look in Daddy's toolshed—but we know Keone won't be there 'cause he hates the noise the tools make. Just as we start jogging out of the back-yard, Laura takes off running across the street in her fluffy pink robe with matching mules.

There sits Keone in the neighbors' front yard among the dead and dying lamb's ears, naked as the day he was born—eating a bag of gingersnaps. We all stand breathless in our paja-mas. Even Daddy looks a little upset. I need more coffee.

Laura grabs the bag of cookies out of Keone's

hand and turns to me and Daddy like we are the criminals she always knew us to be and says,

"Who the hell left the cabinet unlocked so he could get cookies?"

3

I THINK DECLARING YOUR LIFE OUT LOUD MUST BE like drinking too much. You hear people talking about how they made promises to God, Buddha, Vishnu, or whoever that they'd never drink again after they almost drowned drunk in somebody's toilet. But there they are at the next house party, leaning and grinning.

When I look out the window of the Endangered Species Café I feel like I'm in a submarine while it rains all over the planet. I can hear the buses blowing by and taxi drivers using their horns instead of their brakes.

The last time it rained like this I stepped into a Ninth Street pothole that swallowed half my body. But there was Falcone—grinning under a hoodie—standing over me.

"Oh, Scotty, my poor baby girl, did you stumble? My, my—let me help you up before Middle-earth sucks you down there."

Middle-earth wouldn't be so damned bad right now. I'm here at the Endangered because they're serving tofu casserole in the lunchroom and I feel bad for all of us. I'm vegetarian and not ever do I feel tofu anymore. Anyway, the Endangered serves meat; I just don't eat it. So I'm wolfing down wild mushrooms and tomatoes on toasted buttery French bread.

I pledged to eat nothing with a face on it for the rest of my life since I visited that dairy farm last year in my earth science class. Laura, my stepmother, says she respects me for being a vegetarian. Daddy thinks it's something we can bond over. Honestly, though, I'd rather Laura bond with me by buying me a fake ID and taking me and my friends to Vegas.

So Laura makes tofu desserts, tofu tacos, tofurkey, tofu stir-fry, tofu . . . whatever.

I'm tofu screwed at home.

But I've made other pledges that aren't working out like they should.

I haven't learned Kiswahili—they don't offer it at my school.

I haven't stopped buying eight-dollar fashion magazines and drawing spaghetti and french fries on the too-skinny models' mouths.

I haven't volunteered anywhere since those two and a half days at the public library where I was asked to leave in the middle of my shift on the third day. I even heard a librarian tell an aide she thought I was a sociopath. I had refused to remove my big furry purple hat, and that Jack the Ripper book Laura wanted me to pick up fell out of my bag.

But that hurt my feelings.

Misha and Falcone, being my best friends, tried to make me feel better about my crashing of all the library's computers. They took me to the Endangered Species Café for the first time then about a year ago, where I commenced to eat two veggie Reubens, drink four glasses of iced pumpkin-spiced coffee, and inhale a bucket of sweet potato fries. The Endangered Species has a good vibe so I try to have an empty belly when I get there.

Falcone said the librarian was wrong about me being a sociopath *and*—she wore ugly shoes. He also said the library probably feared me because I was a dangerous intellectual. I kinda defended the librarian because she spoke Kiswahili. Misha said someone else probably crashed the computers and the library was covering for them.

I smiled at Misha and Falcone—remembering when we all used to get caught eating paste together underneath the art tables in kindergarten. They even stayed friends with me when I was a bald nine-year-old after Kris Jones perpetuated a particularly nasty chewing-gum crime throughout my hair.

This was so much better. I said the whole thing made me feel stupid and that we should order another bucket of fries.

My life is like tofu—it's what gets added that makes it interesting. It might be good for me, sometimes it's kinda bland and needs hot sauce to spice it up, and most times I complain, silently, that I don't like it, but I think that's normal. I like to whine.

Forget it. I'm late leaving the Endangered for my fifth-period class and if I don't hurry past all these little freshmen looking confused in the hall (still after two and a half weeks) I'll have to go back and beg the secretary in the office for a late pass. And nobody wants that.

ANGELA JOHNSON

4

AFTER SCHOOL ME AND MISHA GO TO KEN'S HIS and Hers for Misha's homecoming dress. She spent two hours last week picking out her favorite one.

"Is it gonna fit?"

"It'll fit."

"I don't know, girl. Can you breathe?"

"Is it important to breathe—much? See the way the fabric flows?" Misha twirls around the dressing room.

The store clerk smiles at her and says, "I think it's almost perfect, but it needs a little tailoring. Your aunt Caroline called earlier to say it might. She says most of your tops need to be let out. Said she might drop by."

Me and Misha look at each other and roll our eyes at the same time, then start to giggle. Misha's aunt Caroline dropping by isn't going to be a good look for anybody. And it gets to be so funny we end up howling on the floor. It would have been better if the store clerk had told Misha she'd be rounding up flying monkeys to help her try on clothes and make suggestions. We keep laughing till it's just us snorting and hiccuping, then finally we get serious. Kind of.

"What she means, Misha, is they can let it out in the bodice or you'll end up passed out with your dress over your head near the punch bowl."

Misha shoots me a cross-eyed look.

"I should've asked Nick to do this with me. Only Falcone probably would have found out about it, been pissed at me. He hates missing the fun."

"Ah, you should have asked Nick. I miss him." And I think that when they broke up we were supposed to act like Nick never existed. I guess we're showing real loyalty to Nick by staying friends with him.

"Tell that to Falcone. You know how he is . . ."

Misha just shrugs and twirls again.

"That boy needs to stop being bitter about the breakup," she says.

"It looks like for now, bitter it is."

"Maybe he needs a new boyfriend."

"Don't even think about it—he hates people messing with that."

"Damn—he's such a boy."

Misha, being hardheaded, won't let the salesgirl make arrangements to have the dress altered—until her aunt Caroline blows in. . . .

Imagine a tropical bird who speaks in declarations and won't take no for an answer, wears long dangling earrings, and always carries an umbrella, antacids, a copy of "Letter from the Birmingham Jail," and nicotine chewing gum (thirty-year cigarette habit) while trying to control her niece.

She walks in and says "Girls" and she's off and around the entire store with the clerk having to duck, dodge, and run to keep up with her.

Misha stands still in the lacy black dress.

"Homecoming does fall on Halloween this year," she says.

I just giggle nervously and pull at my ear like when I was little and had to pee. Caroline rolls her eyes and ignores the dress.

If Falcone was here he would make Misha use her common sense and maybe make a deal. But more than likely he would just crack on the Caroline situation till Misha laughed so hard, ultimately passing out in the dressing room— probably with her dress over her head. But I'm not up to sparring with Aunt Caroline about the homecoming gown. I still have Misha's back, though, if it gets real ugly and puffed sleeves get involved.

Caroline keeps running around the shop wrapping Misha in a tape measure saying "No, no, no, and no" to everything, especially the black lace.

I'm so happy that Misha is even going to homecoming and especially that she will be on the court. We almost had to hide that happy 'cause at first she was going to pass on it. Misha is a feminist and the thought freaked her out. Plus she had an idea the uptight coordinator of the homecoming court might say something about her dreads. But that didn't happen. She did frown up at Misha's tattoo of the earth on roller skates, though.

She said, "A bit of theatrical makeup on your shoulder should cover that up."

To be continued . . .

Angela Johnson

5

IT'S BEEN A LONG DAY. I STARTED OFF TIRED FROM helping to wrestle my naked autistic brother back across the street this morning. And I swear, about eight or nine neighbors walked past, but only one looked at our pajama-clad family with the naked cookie-eating seven-year-old.

She'd smiled and asked how Keone was today.

When Laura said, deadpan, "Naked and eating off-limit cookies," the woman just kept smiling, then walked past us while Keone kept trying to get the gingersnaps out of Daddy's hands.

So I have to ask myself (while I sit cross-legged under a bunch of silk skirts as I watch Misha sulk in a sea of taffeta) if my brother is living a naked life in the neighborhood none of us are aware of. I mean—is he some kind of naked phantom running in and out of our house, eating cookies, sitting in the neighbors' gardens when Laura is busy writing? Is Keone living a secret cookie-filled life none of us know anything about? The thought makes me smile while the taffeta starts getting on my nerves.

In the end I text Falcone. I know his soccer match should be over by now 'cause it seems like we've been in Ken's His and Hers for days. I ask him to come save Misha from having to end up on oxygen at the homecoming dance, to stop Caroline from having Misha go to the dance in a chastity belt and flannel gown, and to help stop what feels like a serious headache from knocking me to the ground.

He finally strolls into the dress shop, messenger bag, dressed in black, with a soft smile on his face—which means we won the soccer match. It takes about thirty seconds of him watching Misha twirl around—still—in the dress she wants before he says, "Girl you look good. But I wonder why anyone would buy a dress that only made them look good from the waist down? Is there a reason you wanted the top half of the dress to make you look like a sausage in a casing? Anyway, I guess that makes sense 'cause the dance falls on Halloween. You could just put a banner on the dress with the words 'Jimmy Dean Sausage' running across it."

The clerk covers her laugh up with a cough, Caroline laughs out loud but puts down the granny dress she was loving, and Misha makes arrangements to get the dress tailored.

Falcone hands me two ibuprofen and a bottle of water that he takes from the pocket of his backpack. He looks at Misha, Misha looks at me, and I look at Falcone right before we all crack up.

We walk out the door and head up the street. Everybody's hungry and the best food on the block is at the Endangered. As we walk by the music shop Misha smiles, stops, and presses her face against the window, then taps at it. A brown-haired dude is in the window reaching for a music book.

He smiles back bigger at Misha.

"Who's that?" I ask.

Falcone is on his phone ignoring us both.

Misha presses her face closer to the window and the boy in the window does the same towards her. Uuuuummmm, he's cute I guess.

When they've got lips and nose prints all over the window Misha waves bye to the boy in the window and we both run to catch up with Falcone, who's lost in his iPhone.

"Who's that?" I ask again.

"I call him Nougat Boy. Ain't he cute? He's security over at the market."

We get to the Endangered and walk through the door with the bamboo chimes. Falcone has cruelly taken seats over by the huge wooden bear with a top hat on and I am way far from pleased.

I got bear issues.

But when we finally all sit down, Falcone is trying out a new app, and Misha's wondering if she should have the iced mocha, I say again, "Nougat Boy?"

She decides on the mocha then says—"Yeah, Nougat Boy." I don't know much about him or his real name. Or where he lives—but we keep running into each other, so we flirt. We're flirting."

Falcone finally joins the non-app world again.

"Who's flirting?"

"Misha and somebody named Nougat Boy."

Falcone shakes his head at both of us and goes back to his phone.

I get the black bean chili and a pineapple smoothie. Falcone gets the loaded home fries that have so much food other than potatoes in them they come in a huge-assed bowl and are covered in blue cheese. He gets blueberry iced tea to wash it all down. Misha gets a hamburger with everything on it but mushrooms that ends up being bigger than her head, and a root beer float.

Falcone says, "I'm thinking about going to see Gina."

I smile.

There are four things I remember about Falcone's sister, Gina.

On Falcone's fifth birthday she drew an animal on the belly of each and every kid at his party. I've looked at the video and there were nine of us.

Once, when she was walking Falcone, Misha, and me to the park, she chased a kid who knocked an old lady down on his bike but kept going. She made him cry. He was taller than her and might not even have been a kid.

Third, she used to let me go into her closets and put on anything I wanted. She had beautiful clothes. But it's the scarves I remember. The colors, the textures, the smell of lavender and fruit spice. Then I'd put on a fashion show for anybody who'd look. But really it was for Gina.

But most importantly Gina Alguero was the first person to ever let me drink coffee. Okay, it was a teaspoon of coffee, a cup of milk, and so much sugar the spoon could stand up. But it was pumpkin coffee. I was in love from then on. Nobody could tell me she was not the most fabulous woman in the whole world. And anyway—I was looking for a mom then because mine had gone into a hospital and never come home.

Gina didn't even walk. She glided . . . in sandals or pumps, tennis shoes or flats. But my favorite shoes she had were a pair of silver thong sandals with pearls inset all around them. They were shoes from heaven. Falcone's dad told me years later they were shoes from a local department store. But I didn't believe him. When I asked Gina she just smiled.

When Gina left, Falcone slept in her room for over a month and wouldn't let his dad put him back into his room. He says anytime his dad even looked like he'd bring the subject up he'd hold his breath.

"Yo—do you believe my old man would

fall for the holding my breath thing?" Falcone laughs.

Misha shakes her head, "You were so wrong. Making your poor dad go through that after Gina moved out."

"Hey, I'd do it again if it would make Gina move back. Yeah I would!"

Misha and I look at him.

"I believe it," I say.

Falcone leans back against the orange booth. He looks at a few of the old black-and-white pictures on the wall and drinks his blueberry iced tea to help push down the loaded home fries.

"True dat. Right now I'd take my sixteen-year-old ass, inhale and hold it, then stand in the middle of the living room floor—cause it's got carpet and I won't get a head injury. I was a serious extortionist when I was little. Papi gave me anything I wanted when he thought I would suffocate to death holding my breath. He'd be all . . . 'Oh shit!' With that look on his face like he had when I came out to him. But then he'd be promising to take me to see a soccer match or make empanadas or go to the zoo. Now he'd probably wing me the car keys and his debit card he'd be so desperate."

I say, "I love your father and again—you are so wrong."

Misha just keeps shaking her head.

Falcone puts his tea aside and starts eating his home fries and dipping them in my bowl of black bean chili. We know Falcone is crazy about his dad too, so he just smiles.

"I miss Gina," I say.

We all know she only lives four hours away. But we all know her husband is an idiot and that four hours might as well be four days. "We should go see her. Just get in the car and forget that her husband is probably in his office somewhere pulling the wings off of insects or squeezing puppies too tight."

Falcone smirks.

Misha eats more fries.

I take out my phone and start to map the directions to Gina's house, but then I go into a daydream. I'm suddenly overcome by the smell of lavender and spices. I'm five again, stumbling through Falcone's house in Gina's long skirts and scarves. She's talking on the phone, laughing and wrapping more scarves around me. And it doesn't really matter that it's years and years later I'm feeling all this again in an orange booth at the Endangered Species.

6

"OKAY, WHAT LIE AM I GOING TO TELL PAPI TO get the car? He can't know we're driving four hours—even to see Gina. He prays every time I get the car keys in my hand to go around the corner and up the street to the bodega. If he's so nervous about me driving—why'd he let me get a license anyway?"

"And that along with him knowing you are probably lying about where you're going . . ." Misha hiccups.

Falcone's dad believes the lies Falcone tells about being sick, but those are usually the only lies Mr. Alguero falls for. Falcone has gotten out of school and other things he didn't want to do by faking diseases that haven't been seen on the planet in hundreds of years, or at least not in East Cleveland. . . . He even tried to convince his dad he had scurvy once.

No shame, this boy—I swear.

Falcone looks at Misha. "Time for the story to be about you. Your family is way crazy."

Misha kicks him underneath the table, but grins. "What did that woman on TV say? She doesn't ask people if their family is crazy, she just asks what side are they craziest on."

"No buts, Misha," I say. "I wanna see Gina. Time to pull out one of your wack relatives whose kid has gotten his head stuck in a box or needs to be rescued from a house full of alligators somewhere on the west side. Falcone's dad will let him rescue people."

Misha says, "I don't have to pull any of them out—they're just running around looking for something messed up or crazy to do."

"I like your aunts," Falcone says.

"I like 'em too. I just hope whatever lie we tell to go on a road trip doesn't end with real hurricanes and drought and locusts—you know, my family," Misha says, sighing.

Friendship can be a bitch. Sometimes she rips your best shirt and spills barbecue sauce all over your shoes, then runs all the gas out of your car before stealing your best CD and losing your dog. I hope this trip will be good to Falcone with the least amount of drama, hurricanes, and locusts.

An hour later when we walk past Ken's we see Misha's aunt Caroline running all over the store pointing at dresses, holding more dresses, and shaking her head at anything the dress owner says. When the owner keeps pointing at the dress Misha picked out, Caroline takes the dress from the woman and buries it behind an old-lady opera dress. The saleslady looks at her like she's crazy, but Caroline is just getting started.

Me and Falcone grab Misha's hand and drag her past the window as fast as we can.

It's been a long day by the time I go up to my room and yell into Dad and Laura's room good night. I'm putting on my pajamas when I hear the sound of crunching under my bed. I drop into bed and turn off the light to the smell of peanut butter cookies and the rustling of a bag.

Only so much can happen in a day, I guess. Only so much in a day.

PART 2

Superman

7

KEONE TRACES MISHA'S TATTOO WITH HIS FINGER in an endless loop and it doesn't seem to drive her out of her mind. She's used to him. But I guess the biggest thing is Keone's used to her—so everything is quiet in the living room. He's used to Falcone, too. Falcone sits on the other side of him and is letting him listen to his favorite music on the iPod over and over again.

Misha blows a huge bubble and says, "Jason is getting on my last nerve about the homecoming dance."

Falcone shakes his head and turns the iPod up a little. Keone smiles.

Then Falcone asks, "Why are you taking a date to the dance, Misha? Isn't that a bit old-school with your fists-up power tribe of females? What happened with everybody going as an intermingled pack?"

Misha blows another bubble like she's thinking. She's really doing it because Keone likes the bubbles. But in a minute it's going to be too much stimulation for him. The tattoo, the music, the bubbles. I don't want him to have an overload meltdown so I shake my head at Misha and the bubbles. She knows what I'm getting at and stops blowing them.

"I'm going to the dance with him because everybody in the court is supposed to have a damned escort. I feel like I'm in the fifties."

Falcone laughs, stretches, and looks at me.

"Don't look at me, I can't help this girl. I didn't even know she knew anyone that was born in the fifties. Did you, Misha?"

Misha, who looks like she wants to ignore us, says, "Do I what?"

Falcone cups his hands around his mouth like a megaphone. "Know somebody who was born in the fifties, homecoming princess?"

She hits Falcone with the pillow she's been reclining on, which means she moves her shoulder so Keone can't trace the world anymore. But when he tries, his earbud falls out and the whole quiet thing comes to an end.

Falcone says, "I'll get my boy some cookies."

That chills Keone out and they head out towards the kitchen. Keone follows Falcone, wearing his brand-new pair of Superman pj's. He's had about ten pairs of them since he was three. I hope to hell Superman never gets old with the superhero crowd or Laura is seriously screwed. As it is, after a certain age she's going to have to get somebody to make Keone pajamas.

. . . and good luck with that.

Misha is stretched out on the couch now.

"Why didn't you talk me out of this crazy stunt? Do I even look like I could be a homecoming queen?"

I look at Misha. Occasional bad attitude, stubborn, smart, kind-hearted, creative. When we were in elementary school she used to go up to people and hug them if they looked sad. Most people would have gotten punched, but not Misha. Tattoos, grrrrrl, and always raging she might be—but she's got the heart of an angel and everybody knows it. I'm voting for her and tell her so. But she keeps on complaining. Oh yeah—she's a whiner, like me.

". . . I mean, what's up with this queen stuff? Now that Mrs. Williams woman is seriously on me about my tattoo. She's relentless. I wanna tell her where to go, but if I do, the wrath of Jacks, Martha, Adrienne, and the couple of others I'm too tired to mention will come down on my ass."

I remember how Jacks made sure one of the slumlords in the neighborhood cleaned up his property. He hadn't fixed any of his property in years. She took pictures of the plugged-up plumbing, peeling paint, hole in the roof dripping into the kids' rooms, and the toilet that had backed up in the basement and overflowed. Then she had them blown up poster-sized and sent to the health department and housing people.

The Aunts can be relentless.

"Cover up the tattoo then, Ms. World," I say.

"I'm not covering up my tat. I went through a lot to get it. Fake ID, lying to the Aunts about my whereabouts, having to wear sleeves on fricking hot-ass days for weeks until the scab fell off . . ."

"Yeah, Misha. I know you suffered for somebody else's art."

After raising an extremely inappropriate finger at me, Misha lies down again and keeps whining about how homecoming night is going to be a disaster. Then she complains about Jason, who plays baseball, gets really good grades, and is his class president. Everybody loves Jason.

I say, "Drop him."

Misha sits up and almost screams.

"Why should I drop Jason?"

"Because he's probably a serial killer. Didn't I see him volunteering at the community center last summer and delivering meals to AIDS shut-ins? Didn't he head that drive to raise money to buy books for that library that burned down across town, too? Serial-killing behavior to me . . ."

I get another inappropriate finger gesture from Misha, but she shuts up just as Falcone comes back into the room with a smiling, sugared-up Keone.

Everything goes back to quiet and comfortable.

But after about half an hour Misha says, "I just don't want anybody thinking I like Jason like that. I don't believe in that boyfriend-girlfriend shite. I just worry about staying who I've always claimed to be. I worry about what this all looks like."

I look at Misha.

Falcone looks at Misha.

Falcone looks Misha in the eyes and says, "If

I ever cared about what things looked like I'd never have a life."

Keone ignores everybody in the room and doesn't look Misha in the eye like Falcone does because he's so focused tracing the world on her shoulder.

8

KEONE RUNS AHEAD OF ME ON THE TRAIN. There's not too much I can do about it 'cause my hands are filled with books, packages, and a bag of cookies I try to hide because I don't want him to completely inhale them before we get off the Rapid. I manage to bodycheck him into falling into the seat that's about halfway back in the train. He wants to take the aisle seat but I know better.

I took Keone to his pediatrician's appointment because Laura had a project due for work. I got a rundown of the dos and don'ts of taking Keone to the doctor. That's all done; now we're heading home.

He likes the train, but doesn't get to ride it

very often. Today's the day. He usually puts his feet out in the aisle and it's never good. I put him in the window seat, drop everything in my seat, and try to get it together before the train lurches to a start. I almost make it but lose *Anna Karenina* as she shoots underneath the seat and ends up about three seats ahead of me.

"Damn."

Keone stops looking for his gingersnaps in my backpack and smiles for about a second. But then he goes back to the cookie hunt.

"Need some help?"

Okay—first I have to stop this and say that if this was one of the stories I am always listening to in study hall from some girl who says it's the truth—she swears to God!—I'd look up with my hair all perfect, wearing a hot outfit, and there would stand this dude I'd been wanting to meet forever. I would have noticed him; his friends might have told him that my friends said I liked him. We probably had liked each other for years, but we just never got together.

That little fantasy is over now 'cause it's Kris (of the putting Dubble Bubble gum in my hair, thusly causing me baldness for a very long time) looking down at me holding *Anna* in his hand while Keone has found the cookies, and at the same time managed to take up both the seats and will probably start whining if I try to move him over. I take the book from Kris and glare at a very happy Keone.

"These seats are empty," Kris says, pointing to the ones directly across from my brother.

I take the book from him and stuff it and more of my school papers back in the pack. I make sure the shopping bags won't tip over and surround Keone with them. A man behind Keone with a laptop smiles at me and starts talking to Keone about the train. Keone turns to listen, grins, and keeps eating his cookies. Kris laughs. I mouth a silent *thanks* to laptop man.

I sit down, crazy tired, and Kris sits next to me.

Kris and I don't talk for one and a half stops. Then he makes some crack about how if I'm going to keep monopolizing the conversation he's going to have to move somewhere else. I start to say something but don't because at the same time Keone almost spills his cookies and I don't want to see him eating them off the floor of the train. I get him straightened out again across the aisle.

"So Falcone invited me to go with you all to the dance."

We pass Cedar Hill and I say, "The more

crowded the better. It's good he invited you, I guess; his ex—Nick—was supposed to go. I think the limo is one of those block-long things. If we're going to help climate change along we might as well do it up and get as many people in the thing as possible."

Kris laughs. "So I'm taking the place of the ex-boyfriend?"

"Yeah, so you'll have to be kind, funny, and keep Falcone in line. I mean, since you'll be taking up the space."

Kris laughs again. Then he starts talking about music and the job he's trying to get downtown at a recording studio.

"I didn't know you were that into music."

"Yeah—I write a little. I even do poetry slams. I guess I'm into the writing part, maybe producing."

And in a few minutes I totally forget that he once put so much gum in my hair I almost ended up looking like Uncle Fester. Kris's stop is coming up but he says he'll stay on and help me get Keone home. I look over at Keone who's pressed against the window as it starts to rain and he's holding gingersnaps in one hand and one of my shopping bags in the other. I glimpse his reflection in the window as people get out and Kris stays on. He settles back and starts talk-ing about how his mom made him take up the trumpet—then regretted it.

I'm laughing so hard that I barely hear the brakes screeching when all of a sudden every-thing starts to move in slow motion; the people who were talking about getting a new dog three seats behind us sound like they're going through a tunnel. The man who was working on his lap-top behind Keone looks shocked when it flies up in the air. One second later Kris is laughing and then in another he isn't. I've never seen any-body so still. By now the noise is gone, the lights go off, and everyone is not where they were a minute ago.

I see Keone flying through the air and I think for a minute that he must feel like Superman.

9

THREE NIGHTS BEFORE THE TRAIN, I GOT TAKEN home in a cop car.

I'm afraid of guns. I think people should be afraid of them just like I am. I don't give a good goddamn what gun people say; people shoot people and they've been doing it for years and it's only going to get worse with more people owning guns. People are crazy and no amount of gun safety and gun handling is going to change that.

So because of guns—current events have to be modified at my school. Nothing can be about local news, 'cause locally some people are . . . you know . . . crazy. But I go on the Internet to look up other papers across the country and I find out everybody all over the place is the same kind of nuts.

World hunger, war, climate change, and screaming psychopaths in the streets with signs proclaiming who-knows-what about everybody who doesn't look like them, believe their religion, or supposedly know what the Constitution says. Mostly the signs are misspelled, though, so they can bite me. Why should I give a second of my time to someone who screams about the Constitution but can't spell the word "constitution"?

Sometimes I'd like to find a quiet place in the woods—except there would be bears. And if there are bears in the woods not just content to take your picnic basket and be happy, then you'd have to have guns out there too. A few rounds shot in the air hopefully would scare a picnic-eating bear away.

But I live in a good neighborhood. I wouldn't say safe, 'cause you could seriously get run over by somebody in an SUV late for something. And there's always the fear of candy-selling kids coming to the door while their parents wait at the end of the yard waving and smiling at you to buy their kids' candy so they don't have to make their coworkers do it.

Anyway—if we hadn't fallen asleep on Falcone's couch watching a dumb reality show I would never have had to think about any of this.

I wake up to Misha drooling and Falcone on his cell and it's pitch dark outside. I was supposed to be home two hours ago. We'd been talking about going to see Gina, then I'd eaten something with noodles and cream of mushroom soup that put me in a coma.

"You two up? It's getting late. I'd give you a ride if Papi was home. Let me walk you."

We say . . . "And who's gonna walk you back?"

Falcone looks insulted.

Damn—boys and their egos.

So we walk. Falcone lives about fifteen blocks from my house. Misha lives eight blocks past my house. Once you walk out of the side streets with the family homes, you know you're in the city. (We could stay on the side streets but what fun is that? Dogs barking and people putting their recycling out—boring as hell.) So we all walk past the bodegas, bars, fast food, and we've gotten about two blocks when a cruiser flashes its lights and a siren. Then we hear the loudspeaker tell us to stop.

Misha yells, "Awww hell, mutha, no!"

Jacks. Misha's cop aunt. Well—one of them. And here we are on a school night walking in the dark. Falcone, Misha, and I grab hands, step into the headlights, and smile. Jacks gets out of the car. She's almost six feet tall and wears a plait twisted around her head. She spots us with her flashlight and shakes her head.

"Get in."

We do. And just as we close the door and Jacks closes hers and starts to rant at us about being out—a report comes in over the radio and Jacks takes off.

The difference between the quiet neighborhood Falcone lives in and the quiet neighborhood I live in is about fifteen blocks. But in between for about seven blocks—Dodge.

We pull up to a bodega and Jacks calmly tells us not to even think about moving. How can we? We're in the back of a cop car.

She's walking up to the front door of the convenience store with her hand on her holster when a man runs out yelling. I don't know if it's at her or the world. But he's got a little girl about five or six with him and is carrying a golf club, swinging it. Falcone, Misha, and I are pressed against the back passenger window, watching. Jacks yells at him to put the golf club down, he doesn't, she tells him again, he doesn't. She tells the man to send the little girl over to her; he doesn't do that either. The little girl presses herself against the garbage can by the door of the bodega.

Jacks Tasers the man. The golf club flies back and hits the window of the bodega and a gun falls out of his jacket.

Misha says—"He got off lucky. I just ate her kiwifruit and she lectured me for an hour. I'd have preferred the shock; it's over quicker."

The little girl wears a Winnie the Pooh sweatshirt, pink sweatpants, and high-top tennis shoes that light up. By the time the man has stopped twitching on the sidewalk, there's two more cruisers with flashing lights and loud radios.

Jacks carries the kid towards the cruiser. The little girl looks like she's in a dream. Then Jacks opens the cruiser's driver's door, reaches underneath her seat, and pulls out a bag. She opens it and lets the little girl reach in it to pull out a stuffed pink pig. Then she and Jacks lean against the cruiser, waiting.

Three nights ago I got taken home in a cop car. You never know when you won't just come home at all, I guess.

What would Anna Karenina do? Probably plot some sort of drama not to be found out—but I'm too tired. I really need to get on with that book report.

10

WHAT HAPPENED BEFORE THE TRAIN . . .

I sometimes wonder if everything happened because I can't drive. I've only been trying for a couple of months, but I'm telling anybody who'll listen—I can't drive. And even though Matt from North Coast Driving School is a good teacher—he taught Falcone and Misha (at the same time)—I actually made the man cry. He'd never admit it and he was wearing dark glasses, but I saw the tear running down his face.

It wasn't sweat, either. My dad sweats when I drive with him. I think Matt from North Coast was frustrated with me and didn't know what to do. He secretly knew I was hopeless. That's something they won't cop to. Laura says most driving schools take pride in the fact that they can teach *anybody* to deal with a car.

Well, they can't. And normally none of this would bother me. I mean, I'm not one of those people who dreamed of a car sitting out in the driveway for my sixteenth birthday. I never dreamed of driving down the highway, CD player blasting out whatever . . . I've only ever wanted to drive so I could drive fast in reverse. That's all I ever wanted to do.

There's this picture of my mom sitting in a car waving to my dad—who was taking the picture. What the picture doesn't show is that she'd just scared about five years out of him a few seconds earlier by driving them both in reverse for two blocks through alleys. And she wasn't going slow, either.

I like the way my mom's laughing in the picture. I can't remember what she sounded like in real life, but I like the way her head is thrown back. She looks like she's laughing her head off. Dad said she *was* laughing her head off—at him. She'd scared him in the alley. He couldn't believe how fast she could drive backwards.

When I was ten he framed the photo for me. It sits on my bedside table. I've been wanting to drive backwards ever since. But try telling that to

Matt from North Coast Driving School, who only wants to teach me how to stay on the road, obey signs, stop at the right times, not speed, and finish the course as a responsible driver. Sooooo . . . It's hard for me to stay on the road because they don't make cars skinny enough—I think. It's all right if you have a Mini Cooper, but normal cars are just a little too wide. The manufacturers need to do something about it.

The sign-obeying is just plain hard. STOP, CHILDREN AT PLAY, MERGE, ROUGH SHOULDER (okay, I didn't get what that meant at first— but totally knew there probably weren't people standing around near the road putting lotion on their shoulders). None of this made me want to drive, but all of it made me want to just drive backwards.

So I'm keeping my bus pass and will just get used to walking a few blocks to catch the Rapid like I always have. Mass transit is good for the planet. It's also good for anybody who might have to be on the road when I'm driving. So I'm thinking about not being a driver. It's a way big decision to make before you're sixteen years old—but hey. Maybe I'll change my mind.

I decide to talk to Falcone about it. He's sitting with Jason, DJ, and Kris. I'd like to say I've forgiven Kris. Well—I'd like to say that, but it would be a big-assed lie.

I sit down beside him and pretend he's not there.

Falcone eats pizza and says, "Want some, Scotty?" when he sees I'm not eating anything. "There's not any tofu anywhere on the crust."

Jason, DJ, and Kris look at Falcone, then me.

"What tofu?" Kris says. "Where?"

"There isn't any," I say.

Kris gets all confused like the conversation has suddenly been dubbed in French and the subtitles are gone.

Falcone eats more pizza and with his mouth full says, "No tofu today, dude."

But now Kris is confused and a little bit scared.

"Yo, I eat in this cafeteria every day and they have never and I repeat never served tofu here."

I guess since I've had that bald-headed gum thing hate going on for Kris all these years I've never really sat back and looked at him. A lot of girls would think he was hot. Pretty brown eyes, tall, works on the school paper. And he tries to be nice to me even though I psychopathically love to carry grudges and won't give him a chance to get too close to me. I still fear hidden gum.

And now he claims to not know he's been eating tofu (cleverly disguised as everything) in his beloved school lunches. But this pizza has real porky pig on it.

Now a good person would just drop it. You know, people have food issues. Some food issues will never be fixed. Misha can't eat mushrooms because of the texture, my dad can't eat cranberry sauce because he was frightened by a beet thinking it was a slice of cranberry sauce when he was Keone's age at Thanksgiving, and, well—we all know Keone's thing. It shouldn't be allowed to be called food unless it's a cookie.

This is going to be too easy. Wrong, but easy.

I could now avenge myself for months of people in stores saying, "What a cute little boy." Or whispering when I had a skirt or dress on, "Is that little boy dressed as a girl?"

It's funny. All I sat down to do was tell Falcone my driving days would be over and when the bus or trains weren't running he'd have to be my ride for life. Now this wonderful opportunity has presented itself.

I smile at Kris—you know, like the Grinch.

Falcone, DJ, and Jason shake their heads at me and start talking about algebra. Kris knows something is up, then. His eyes get all wide and he's looking at his slice like it might attack him. He even pushes it away from him a little. I am seconds from the you've-been-eating-tofu-instead-of-(everything) attack when he says, "I guess I need to grow up. If they've made some of the meals out of tofu—I ate 'em. What's the big deal, huh?"

Then Kris smiles at me and asks if I want to join the school paper.

Life's like that. You go along plotting (even with only a minute lead time), hoping, and there it is—plans destroyed. So I decide to spend the rest of my lunchtime up in the earth science room where Ms. Bridges meets with the Greenpeace kids.

There's only about six of them, but I sit in the back of the room and listen as they talk about saving the oceans, and whatever comes with that. I have mad respect for anybody trying to protect the world from the worst of us.

But I'm still trying to navigate the streets of East Cleveland without ever having a license. I have to take Keone to the pediatrician today. I think we'll take the train.

PART 3

If I Could Tell
What I Wanted

11

IT'S LIKE ALMOST EVERY MOVIE YOU'VE EVER SEEN when someone who's been involved in some kind of horrible crime, personal tragedy, or catastrophe shows up. The people part like biblical waters. (At least I think that's what happened.) I spent one summer going to Sunday school with Troy Waters because we always went for ice cream with her parents afterwards.

I got a cavity and no real information that summer 'cause I was too busy coloring the apostles and trying to stay within the lines. I loved the rainbow stickers the Sunday school teacher gave me.

So now I've had four days of looking out the window and going to visit Keone, who's in a coma. I hate the way the doctors keep saying his brain is just taking a vacation. How the hell do they know it hasn't just moved out of the country and is never coming back? After all, it is Keone's already complicated beautiful brain. This doesn't make anything easier. Vacation my ass.

I got off easy with just a severe deep bruising on my right knee and leg, basic body aches, and almost no memory of the train crash. Two other kids who had been on the train from our school died. Now walking through the halls is almost like trying to find a seat on the train, except everyone is watching instead of reading, looking out the window, or listening to iPods. People either drop their eyes when they see you coming or smile at you like you could go off at any minute.

And all anybody wants to ask—but they don't—is the truth about why Kris and I were on the train together.

I thought the grief counselors would be gone by the time I got back to school. But I've never been that lucky. I never thought that I'd be part of the reason we'd have them in the school anyway. All I had to do was tell him I didn't need help with Keone. That's what I should have said. That's all I had to say.

Coulda, shoulda . . .

Misha and Falcone show up at the end of each of my classes and walk me through the crowds. By the middle of the day teachers are letting me out five minutes before class breaks so I don't have to walk through the sea of faces and they don't have to see mine. By the end of the day I don't think I remember anything anybody said to me. I just remember that at two o'clock Falcone's ex-boyfriend Nick showed up at my locker, took my backpack and me by the hand, and drove me home.

He played baroque music on a CD and didn't try to talk to me.

I love him and I wish he and Falcone would get back together.

"You're home now."

Nick walks me into the house and gets me situated on the couch. Laura texted me that her and Dad would be at the hospital. I watch Nick go in the kitchen to make me some tea. His hair is blond and burgundy this week. I used to wear his clothes—we're the same size. He laughs when nobody else laughs, goes camping (which I don't get), and used to *love* Falcone. Me and Misha had to basically give him up in the divorce. Not totally, but mostly.

"This is good and hot."

"I remember you used to say that about someone I know."

He shakes his head. "Give it up, Scotts. That boat sailed, sank, and got towed."

"But . . ."

"No. It ain't going to happen."

He sits down next to me and I curl up next to him.

"Nicky, it's hard being a child of your divorce and probably the reason somebody is dead."

Nick raises my head with his hand and looks at me and smiles.

"Life bites, baby girl."

". . . and sucks."

Amen.

12

I KEEP READING *ANNA KARENINA* AND DREAMING that my ten-page report on her will magically appear on my laptop tonight. It hasn't happened.

If it had been a perfect fall it would have been about homecoming—whining about homecoming, trying to make money for homecoming. And in my case ignoring the fact that I need to get a dress for homecoming. The pressure is off about a date 'cause we are going as a group; at least I think I might still be going.

But now I just keep reading *Anna Karenina* and taking long walks, limping through the neighborhood and watching the neighbor's lives.

Mr. Sifuentes got hair plugs.

Ms. Rankin's terrier is still a yapper.

Is Mr. Sutley getting taller *and* younger? I'm thinking vampire.

If Mrs. Jacobs puts any more lawn ornaments out, one of her loved ones should have her committed.

I'm loving *Anna*, but just got to the railroad tragedy and had to put the book down. . . .

I keep walking and thinking how Falcone misses his sister. She's been gone for ten years and he's only seen her nine times. Gina always visits Falcone and his dad on Father's Day. This year Falcone's birthday fell on Father's Day—but this was the first time in ten years Gina didn't show.

On all the holidays she goes to her husband's family. So on Easter, Memorial Day, Fourth of July, Labor Day, Thanksgiving, and Christmas she never eats the food Mr. Alguero bakes, grills, or roasts.

For Mr. Alguero, food is love. Gina is missing the love.

She never gets to hang out with Falcone and the rest of us as our music pounds all over the neighborhood.

Now my family invites the Algueros over. Misha and her four hundred and fifty aunts invite them over too for card playing in their backyard, eating way too much, and—if it's a year that Misha's aunt Jacks made wine—line-dancing and playing drunken volleyball until people crawl home exhausted and happy.

When Gina didn't come home this past summer she sent Falcone an e-mail. She never calls. I don't even think she has a cell phone. That makes Falcone's dad crazy. He worries she'll be on the road broken down somewhere and won't be able to call a tow.

What he doesn't know is that besides coming to visit them once a year, Gina doesn't drive anywhere else. The car she brings to visit is always a rental. She doesn't have her own car in Cincinnati and she's never allowed to drive her creep husband's unless he's in it. She told Falcone and made him promise not to tell their father. I have a feeling there's a whole lot of things Gina is keeping from Falcone, too.

I miss her. I shouldn't because I was only five when she packed up her beautiful clothes, got in her blue Sunbird, and took off to college. I shouldn't even remember that much about her—but there are pictures and videos she took with us.

Instead of coming back home for Thanksgiving the year she left for college, she sent Mr. Alguero and Falcone a picture of her standing beside a fountain in a lace dress with a man who looked like one of the models I always draw eating french fries. And then she was gone—except one visit a year and three e-mails a month to her father and brother.

It's like the laughing, lavender-scented, scarf-wearing girl who held me till I cried myself to sleep disappeared into a mist four and a half hours away. But the one thing we always knew was nobody was supposed to visit Gina. In her e-mails she'd say her husband Aaron didn't like company.

Well none of us like him.

We only met him once. Mr. Alguero said Aaron had a look on his face that made you think he smelled something bad.

All I could think was bad karma was all around him.

Misha thought he could use a good shake.

Falcone never says a word.

Anna K.'s been sitting on my lap this whole time and I'm hoping it's filled with the truth about love and other disasters.

13

I'VE WALKED AROUND THE BLOCK TEN TIMES TODAY.
On my street—

Number 78 needs to stop letting their dog pee in the front yard.

Number 71 needs to take their recycle bins in; they're full of leaves.

Number 59 doesn't have any curtains, but has a scarecrow dressed in a wedding dress in the front yard. (Their shout-out to Halloween, I guess.)

Number 46's wife must have kicked him out, because their yard is filled with men's clothes: over shrubs, in the frog fountain, in the flower beds. And his car is filled with clothes. I think he slept in it last night.

Number 35 keeps an illegal llama (really) in the back of their yard and he (not the llama) stands on the side of his house in the evening smoking bud.

Number 26 started smoking cigarettes again and her husband still hates it 'cause she's basically living outside on her porch, plaid throw, magazines, coffee cups, and CD player and her—in a haze of smoke. I hope she's getting enough air.

I read somewhere that people don't take in enough oxygen in their daily lives. I've decided to inhale and exhale dramatically at least five times a minute. It takes practice. I used to catch myself holding my breath and I didn't even know why. Most of us are missing some serious oxygen because something that's supposed to be natural turns out not to be for a lot of people.

You just have to breathe and mean it.

So on my ninth trip around the block I empty all the leaves out of number 71's recycle bins. I leave the leaves on the devil strip for the city to suck up, and take the recycle bin down the driveway and leave it on the side of the house with number 71's garbage cans and water-hose reel and dead pots of daisies. Damn—number 71 is way behind on the summer cleanup, and they have a ground-hog. I decide it's a she, watching me as I put the bin between the garbage and the hose, because of the smaller ones skittering behind her.

As I get back to the street number 71 is just pulling in to the driveway.

I walk on. Good deeds are supposed to be secret.

I'm just starting my tenth time circling the block for the day when Falcone pulls up.

"Ride, lady?" he says, turning his dad's Marc Anthony CD down (his car, his music, Falcone's dad always says) and throwing some of his junk off the passenger seat to make room for me. And it's a lot of junk Falcone has to throw too. Sometimes I think he's living number 46's life, only no divorce. I see water bottles, books, hoodies, chip bags, socks, a globe, four or five different kinds of shopping bags, a bird-cage (does Falcone have a bird he hasn't told me about?), and two or three soccer balls.

"I got one more time around," I say, leaning into the car still wondering where I'd sit 'cause the seat is still full. ". . . and anyway you don't have the room. I'm half expecting to see Bigfoot roll out the backseat."

Falcone turns Marc Anthony down even lower and squeezes my hand.

"Time to go home, Scotty."

"One more time around," I say, pulling my hand out of his.

Then as I'm backing away a wind comes up and blows leaves down on me and all over Falcone's windshield. I almost forgot until then that fall is my favorite time of year. Bonfires, football games, pumpkins everywhere, being able to walk and have yellow, red, and orange leaves dance in the wind, apple cider . . .

Fall.

Falcone puts his car in drive and follows me, crawling along. He turns Marc Anthony back on, but not as loud as before, as more leaves blow from the trees.

I close my eyes for a few seconds, then walk on, breathless.

ANGELA JOHNSON

14

Twelve o'clock midnight at Paul's Market is the best time to buy food. Misha pushes me in the cart—my knee propped up—and is eating from a carton of Fig Newtons. I'm not really one with the fig, but Misha's addicted. So she munches and pushes me while I point to what I want and she gets it or I stand up in the cart and reach for it.

"Jacks has written down heavy cream," I say, reading from her list. "Does that mean whipping cream or half and half?"

"Get the whipping cream; at least it has 'cream' in the name. We'll probably be wrong but I'll just whine that she's always working me like a dog so why does she expect me to read her mind too?"

"Uh-huh."

I get the whipping cream, strawberries, blueberries, little round shortcakes, and a gallon of milk. Jacks get cravings (non-pregnant ones) and me and Misha are always willing to borrow her car and take care of it.

The most fun, though, is gliding through the supermarket on wheels. Nobody cares on the midnight shift. Security—or Al, who hits on any woman who comes through the door—only works until ten. After that is a dude with long curly brown hair who looks about twelve only real tall, is always eating candy bars, and never hears anything because he's got his iPod cranked up and is always reading *X-Men* comic books. Maybe even the same one for all I know.

Misha rolls her eyes towards Nougat Boy, as she calls him. He catches her looking at him and he smiles at her. Then he speaks to her. She stands there listening to him talk about . . . whatever.

I get out of the cart like the hurt soul that I am. The girl with the huge 'fro at the counter smirks at me, turns, and keeps talking to the bag boy. I start wandering the aisles of Paul's and it's like a food dream with jazz playing and bright ultraclean floors. You can't really hear the music in the daytime at Paul's.

And then I go down the cookie aisle. . . .
Chocolate chip,
peanut butter,
Oreos,
lemon,
oatmeal raisin,
chocolate macadamia,
sugar cookies,
molasses cookies,
and gingersnaps.

The next afternoon I go through the double doors of the hospital, up the elevator, and turn right towards Keone's room. Pediatrics is always on lockdown. I sign in and the door clicks open. I head towards his room, walking past a mural that runs the length of the hall—rabbits, bears (why?), and other woodland creatures follow me past crying babies, cartoon sounds spilling out of rooms, and parents walking in and out.

Keone has a room by himself at the end of the hall. I walk in with my bags. He's sleeping. Broken and sleeping. His train and plane and automobile books are piled up on the heating vents. He's covered in his favorite comforter— blue and red trains. Laura or my dad must have just left or might even still be here down in the cafeteria because I see new books.

I tiptoe past Keone's bed and pile more books and DVDs onto the register. Then I walk over to his bed and climb in next to him. Keone smells like baby powder. I read to him until I fall asleep and dream about trains too—only it wakes me up in a cold sweat.

I stay about an hour. When I leave I put a bag of gingersnaps on my little brother's bedside table.

I take the bus now.

It's only a block from the bus stop to my house. When I get there I sit on the porch and breathe in the smoky wood odor you only get to smell in the fall. I look down the street towards number 26, who's still on the porch. I see a little red light every now and then. She must be living on her porch now. I sit on our porch swing with my two shopping bags. In a few minutes the porch light flickers off, then on again.

Dad pulls the blinds back, holds them— then lets them go. He opens the door and waits for me to come in. I pick up my bags and go inside. He sits down and watches television.

"How was school and everything else? I didn't get to talk to you last night."

"I was hangin' with Misha while she flirted with Nougat Boy."

"Who? Anyway, did you get what you needed at the store—at midnight?"

"Yeah, Daddy. I did."

"Good, but I'm never happy with you two being out that late. Next time take Falcone."

"Daddy, you're a chauvinist." I say. "I just came back from seeing Keone. Were you there this afternoon?"

"I'm there every afternoon, baby."

I lean over and kiss him on the top of his head like he used to kiss me. Then I take my bags upstairs and head for my room. I almost slip on one of Keone's train books in the hall, then think about telling Laura I'm home. But instead I head towards Keone's room.

I go inside, almost trip on another one of his picture books, turn on the lamp by the door, pick the book off the floor, and put it on his shelf. Then I turn off the light and open one of my handle bags. I walk over, climb into his empty bed. Then I open up a bag of gingersnaps and cry until I can't cry anymore. After a while I fall asleep.

PART 4

Funeral for a Friend

15

I'M ONE OF THOSE PEOPLE WHO DON'T HAVE problems going to funerals. I get up, put on my black dress (Laura says every woman should have one), pull my braided do back in a bun, slide my feet into black ballet flats, and find my dark glasses. Yeah, to me it's the circle of life thing. I don't mind going to a funeral with an almost friend.

No school for me today.

I wait on the porch as the last of the leaves blow off the trees. We had a big-assed wind night before last and it took many of the leaves that weren't ready to go. But I guess that's how it is.

Kris pulls up in a minivan and I limp through a yard of leaves.

"Hey," he says.

"How's it going?" I say, and get in.

He doesn't put the car in gear until I have my seat belt on. I smile 'cause neither of us has to ever say what we're both thinking. Kris pulls away from the curb and drives pretty well considering he's got a broken right arm and a busted right foot. His broken nose doesn't affect his driving, but it makes me wince for him every time we go over a pothole.

"Yo, thanks, Scott. I mean—thanks for doing this with me. I think it's the least we can do, even though my moms had a fit about me driving and wanted to chauffeur us."

"That would have been okay," I say.

"No, it wouldn't have been okay. I've been on medical lockdown. My moms has been following me all over our house. She won't go back to work because she's afraid the school's gonna call because I've passed out or something and she'll be too far away to get to me from her job. My pops works half a mile from my school, but after the divorce there wasn't any trust left. At least on my mom's part. So I leave her alone about going back to work—or she cries."

"Where does she work?"

"Avon Lake."

"Yeah, well she's right about that. That's almost a day's trip in the middle of the afternoon—even on the freeway. And if you take the surface streets it might take a week."

Kris nods his head, smiles at me, and gets on Cedar Road heading towards Shaker.

I hate that the wind is blowing fallen leaves away. I lean back 'cause I realize I've been sitting at attention—tense. My knee hurts. At the last minute I put the brace on, otherwise it would give out. Walking helps—round and round my block. I go to rehab at a gym on Euclid Ave. But I want to work out myself.

I don't want to be one of those people who can tell when it's going to rain like my aunt Minnie. Of course I don't want to be anything like Aunt Minnie 'cause she chews tobacco, wears housedresses to weddings, and won't answer her phone during football season 'cause she says she can't be talking to people wasting her time when she's praying for the Browns to go to the Super Bowl.

Uh-huh. Aunt Minnie.

We pass the Fairmount mansions, make a few turns, and end up at Highland Park Cemetery. There's a line of cars already there and people are just getting out to walk towards the grave site. I get out of the car, lift up the handle of the side door, and it slides open. I get Kris's crutches and take them around to him.

He smiles and all I can think about is how his nose must hurt. I got out of it all with a wrenched, bruised knee and leg and a few other body bruises.

We walk towards the sea of black for the funeral of the man who had been on his laptop that afternoon. As we get closer people start to part the way for the boy in the casts and the limping girl beside him. A man in a black suit carrying an umbrella finds two chairs for us to sit behind the family.

So here we are, broken, bruised, and wrenched. And here we are sitting through a service for the man who was the last person to talk to my little brother—before both their lives changed.

The pastor starts talking and Kris relaxes against the black plastic chair. I lean a little closer to him 'cause you never know when he might need a shoulder. And like his mom I don't want to be too far away 'cause I feel guilty that he stayed on the train for one stop too many to help me with Keone.

There's crying all around us, and even

though I never really mind funerals I wouldn't have come if it hadn't been for Kris. You have to step up if it's something for a friend.

Kris drops me off and pulls off blowing his horn. As I get out of the car a little kid flies by me. His sister is chasing him down the sidewalk and he's covered in leaves. I smile at him but he doesn't look back because a getaway will always trump hello.

Then I wake up. The dream was as close to Kris's funeral that I ever got to be.

16

I SAY IT'S LIKE HICCUPS YOU CAN'T GET RID OF.

Falcone's sitting at the foot of my bed with his iPod, and Misha is kicked back on the bean-bag. I don't want to complain because they are my serious boy and girl—but they never let me out of their sight anymore. The hiccups part isn't them though. It's how everything was going and how it is now. Hiccup.

One minute I was on a train with a boy who I'd ignored since he put gum in my hair when we were six, the next minute I was laughing with the boy who put gum in my hair, and the minute after that he's lying three feet away from me and won't ever go home again.

Half of Keone's bones are broken.

I got bruises and a twisted knee.

Life is stupid.

But Misha's on a mission. I've been on one of Misha's missions, and it's not always a safe place to be. But I think she's going on this mission because of me. She wants me to forget. I remind her about the vendetta she has against Mrs. Williams who seems to have an obsession with her tattoo showing at homecoming. She rails against closed minds and the status quo until I think I need a nap.

I'm willing to forget. But I don't think three weeks is time enough to forget a train wreck or reporters calling our house or Laura threatening their lives if they kept calling. Three weeks isn't enough to forget that Keone's little body is lying in a hospital bed broken and the few words he used to say are all gone. Three weeks isn't enough time to wrap my brain around any of it.

Hell—I'd like to take my brain right out of my head and mail it to a water park. Or I'd like to go on a bubble bath and Cheetos vacation.

". . . think we should, Scotty?"

"What?"

Misha inhales and looks at me like I'm a little kid who just had an accident on the floor. She wants to scream, but she knows I can't help myself—at least not right now, anyway.

"Do you think we should what?"

Misha crawls over to the bed and climbs up on the bed next to me. She looks at me, exhales, then hugs me.

Damn. Hugging. I didn't think she'd do that. I thought maybe—I guess I thought I could count on Misha to be more tough love. I didn't expect the hugging. Falcone acts like he isn't even in the room. Too much hugging and sympathy is bound to make him run out the room, down the hall, and out of the door. I feel sorry for him. But mostly I feel real sorry for me right now 'cause all I want to do is not have Misha have that *Oh you poor thing* look on her face.

Damn. Accepting condolence is hard. And painful. And it makes you remember.

Falcone leans back and tries to transport his body someplace else with just the power of his mind and the candy bar he's started eating. Misha and I look at him and start to laugh.

"What?" he says.

"Nothing," I say.

"Nothing," Misha says.

Then we almost roll off the bed laughing.

The sun is starting to set and it does its last dance through the few red and orange leaves on the trees. Falcone isn't in the room anymore, but I hear him downstairs talking to my dad. They both laugh out loud about something. Misha is snoring beside me and has curled up with my stuffed lamb, Mario. Earlier she'd looked all over my room for a teddy bear.

There aren't any.

Bears are technically beautiful—but people are basically dumb about them. I don't understand the obsession with giving children stuffed creatures that in real life can rip your head off and eat you if you happen to be stupid enough to follow them or surprise them in nature.

And anyway there was a bear that actually showed up in the 'burbs (five minutes from my house) a few weeks ago and ripped the siding off a house to try to get at some dirty dishes in the sink. The window was open and I guess the bear smelled the leftovers. True story. All the fast-food places must have been closed. And even though there are more people injured by dogs, dogs can't rip the doors off your house then drag you bleeding into the woods. And let's face it, the only harm a lamb can do is if someone chokes on it with mint sauce.

Thus, Mario.

·   ·   ·

Misha says in the shadow of my room, "Do you wanna go to Kris's grave?"

I say, "I thought I had; then I woke up."

"Huh?" she says.

"I thought I had. Well, not really. I dreamed I went to a funeral with Kris. He was hurt and had a broken leg and arm—I should have known it was a dream."

"We never know when we're dreaming."

"I should've known. It was too strange. But it was too real when it was happening. I was so glad to see him. I knew everything was okay 'cause he was well enough to think about somebody else."

Misha says again, "It's okay, Scotty, we never know when we're dreaming."

"I don't think I'm ready to go see Kris's grave."

"Okay. But when you're ready, I'll go with you."

"Cool."

"Yeah."

Misha flies Mario through the air, and I smile in the almost dark.

17

LATELY I CAN'T SIT DOWN.

If I'm in a chair more than two minutes I'm jumping up to look out the window or checking the thermostat because I feel too hot or too cold. I stare off into the kitchen and decide I want a snack but when I sit at the counter making a sandwich or whatever I leave it before I finish making it.

My body is in one place while my mind is in another.

I've been limping around the neighborhood and trying to ignore the old folks' concerned looks when I tell them I'll be back—whenever. That is what brought me to Rodney's Comics.

Whenever.

Two blocks from my house and a place I never went into. Rodney's. Home to comic-book and graphic-novel lovers who just happen to be, on a Saturday, every guy in my school who probably at some point wanted to date Misha but would have tripped over his tongue, feet, and a staircase while trying to ask her.

And if only the poor fools would actually ask her out . . . They are Misha's kind of guys. Geeky, probably smart, scared of girls, and have discretionary income they use to buy reading material instead of bomb-making implements. So when I walk in, all eyes are on me 'cause I'm probably not their usual kind of customer. I got a pastel hoodie on and smell like expensive per-fume (which I put on in a moment of boredom while rifling through Laura's toiletries in the bathroom). Actually, I've been sneezing from it since I left home.

But now I'm just looking. And I know it's going to be okay when the bearded man behind the counter drops his eyes and doesn't ask me what I'm looking for. My kind of place.

So I peruse the tables of plastic-covered issues of *X-Men*, *The Avengers*, *The Amazing Spider-Man*, *The Incredible Hulk*, *Batman*, *Wol-*

verine, and *Superman*, and it feels so good not to know anything about what I'm looking at. I can move along the tables and take in the huge posters on the walls of mutant superheroes and listen to the way the guys who lean against the far walls and squat along the shelves talk about the comic-book world.

Here it's okay for my body not to be with my mind.

Until.

"So, are you into old-school DC or more into graphics?"

Again, my mind, of course, is not with my body. It's halfway across the room staring at a poster of a warrior woman with a sword who in real-assed life wouldn't be able to walk because her waist is about two inches in circumference and her chest is about a quadruple-D cup. You gotta love the artist's imagination—and his probable sadness at never realizing his dream. I turn around to see smiling lips, laughing eyes, and hair all over the place. Nougat Boy. Comic book in place, but no candy bar 'cause there's about ten signs saying no food in the store.

One says, DON'T EAT FOOD IN THIS STORE SO I DON'T HAVE TO PROVE TO YOU THAT I'M THE ASSHOLE EVERYBODY SAYS I AM.

Rodney's is my new favorite place, featuring comic books I know nothing about, deformed superheroes, a reading public, rude signs, and a strange smiling boy who asks me questions— that again sound like an alien language.

I smile back at Nougat Boy, who finishes asking me about comics in about ten seconds, then asks me how my knee is, then how life in general is treating me—and finally, "How's your friend Misha?"

I smile my *you just won a shopping spree and can bring a friend* smile at Nougat Boy. My mind and body become friends again and it comes to me while I'm telling him about how Misha is a saint and doesn't date and saved a basket of puppies when we were eight—I can make something good happen and I won't have to think about myself for a while.

I'll get Misha and Nougat Boy together 'cause if somebody doesn't get all up in their business all they're ever gonna do is flirt with each other.

The universe is cruel, but it doesn't mean you can't bring about some happiness for some of the poor creatures who have to live in it.

18

Awwww, HELL.

I forgot Misha is going to homecoming with Jason. How am I going to change her destiny if she keeps making plans that have nothing to do with mine?

I say over the phone, "What about Nougat Boy?"

Misha sighs and says, "He's a musician, plays the piano and speaks Spanish fluently because he spent the first seven years of his life in Mexico City with his dad."

I guess they did flirt and talk.

Jason asked her weeks ago to go to homecoming with him as friends. But she says she just invited Nougat Boy over to her house and I have to come with Falcone later for dessert. I start to tell her I saw him at Rodney's and gave him her phone number, but she says,

"He just called me. What were you doing in Rodney's?"

"Trying to mess with the universe," I say.

"Huh?"

"Nothing. I'm just glad you two are hookin' up."

"It's not a hookup. He's just strange and I like him."

That's good enough for me.

Later I tell Falcone we have to go to Misha's. He says, "What the fu . . . ," just as his dad walks into the room.

"Watch your mouth," Mr. Alguero says, and heads out the front door with a bird feeder.

"Sorry, Papi," Falcone says to his papi's back, then to me, "Why I gotta come to dessert? And how the hell did she hook up with somebody called Nougat Boy?"

"His name is Thelonious."

Falcone drops to the couch and kicks a soccer ball across the room that almost takes out a picture of him when he was a baby and a vase sitting underneath it.

"What the hell kind of name is Thelonious?"

"Monk."

"Huh?" Falcone says looking confused.

"He was a jazz musician."

"Okay," Falcone says, still looking confused.

"He played piano," I say. I looked it up—and since Falcone is getting on my last nerve I decide to give him the full bio.

"He died in 1982 and . . ."

Falcone smirks. "Stay off Wikipedia—girl."

"Shut up—boy."

"Nawww, you first."

I grab a pillow and think about clocking him with it but Mr. Alguero walks back through the door, smiles at me, and asks if I'm staying for dinner.

Yes—I will.

"So you two can set the table, then."

I like Falcone's house. It's tumbled but put together. And you'd never know a woman doesn't live here. It isn't what you might expect—a gym ('cause Falcone and Mr. Alguero are jocks). There are always cut flowers in the house and it is seriously clean, but comfortable.

"So you're going, right?"

Falcone puts the forks beside the plates, then remembers the napkins. He goes over to the sideboard and gets three cloth napkins. We always use paper napkins at our house 'cause Keone goes through them like everything . . .

I sit at the table and start to cry. I do it a lot

now. All of a sudden and real hard I'll just start crying like a baby.

Falcone moves over to my side of the table, puts the last napkin down, then wraps his arms around me. I cry so much I get a real snotty nose—he hands me one of the napkins. I start laughing, but don't use it.

I know Falcone wants to run or get on his iPhone or pretend he's somewhere else. It's the crying and sadness that freaks him out. I think it's a boy thing—but that would be sexist, although it's probably true. So he stands there and holds me while I drain almost every drop of liquid out of my body. In the end Falcone leaves me for a second and comes back with a gigantic piece of paper towel.

"Better?" he asks.

"Yep. Thanks for the paper towel."

"No prob."

I start to think how sweet Falcone can be. He'll even give you the last bite of his ice cream cone if you look sad enough, and I get sad a lot when there's ice cream. Falcone deserves to share ice cream with someone he loves and can share clothes with. *What to do, what to do?*

I blow my nose for what I hope is the last time and still keep thinking of Kris and Keone and the new girl who had just been here two days and knew no one at school before she died. By the time Mr. Alguero has come into the dining room carrying what smells like empanadas, I'm ready to be normal again—whatever that is these days.

We sit down to eat and Mr. Alguero starts talking about the boat he's fixing up so he and Falcone can go fishing together.

"She's a beauty—heh, son?"

Falcone nods with his mouth full of empanadas and smiles between bites at his Papi. The only thing Falcone loves more than his father and soccer (and once upon a time, Nick) is fishing.

He told me once he didn't know if it was because you had to be quiet, or if it was that everything smelled and felt better in the early morning, or if it was the company of his dad as they sat in the boat unwrapping egg, pork, and onion sandwiches from wax paper and eating them, while birds flew overhead and the water rippled away from their boat.

Who'da thunk it?

Cool Falcone, all dressed in black, street and with an ex-boyfriend who would get hives when he had to leave the city.

I'm still sniffing a little so Mr. Alguero starts telling funny stories about fixing up his boat. I figure he probably heard me crying while we were in the kitchen.

I laugh harder than I have in a long time at Mr. Alguero's boat stories. And by the end of dinner I almost forget that I had a mini meltdown. Me and Falcone start clearing the table. His papi gets on the phone and leaves the room.

"So are you going to Misha's or not with me?"

"I'll go, Scotts," he says.

"Good, 'cause I didn't think you were gonna answer me."

"Yeah, well I would have if you hadn't started crying."

"Whatever, Halloween's coming—I wanted to scare you," I say.

"I gotta say that I feel like I'm going behind my boy Jason's back. I mean—I know they're only going together because Misha needs a date. And let's face it, Jason is probably the only dude who won't rip her dress, get drunk, and start a fight or make a move on some other girl in front of her."

"Okay—yeah, that's probably true."

"She should still talk to Jason. I don't know, I mean he might feel like he's being dissed if he found out about Nougat Boy—"

"Thelonious."

"Yeah, yeah, Thelonious."

"True. I'll say something to her about it."

We go into the kitchen and pile the dishes up on the counter.

"I'll wash," I say.

Falcone starts running the hot water in the sink and puts in too much dish soap.

"I wish Papi would get a dishwasher."

"He has one," I say.

"Yeah—that would be me."

I pass the dishes to Falcone to dry and we don't talk for the next twenty minutes. And that's how I know who I'm close to. If I can be in a room with somebody and be comfortable enough not to say anything for that long . . . we're tight.

I pass the rest of the dishes to Falcone.

"Thelonious, huh?"

"Yeah Falcone, Thelonious."

"Okay, I just have to get used to it."

"We got used to your name."

"What does that mean, girl?"

I stick my hand in the last of the soapy water

as it goes down the drain, then turn and look at Falcone.

"You're named after a predator *bird*, Falcone."

". . . and your ass is named after the engineer on the *Star Trek Enterprise*."

I laugh until I cry a whole different kind of tears.

I've been thinking a lot lately about baked goods, boys, Cupid—and how if he lived now he'd be on antidepressants. Sometimes you just have to move things along. Love is hard to get back sometimes, but I'm motivated. I find myself looking through old photographs of summers gone by but stop when I see an amazing picture I've never seen before. Laura or my dad must have taken it.

My heart skips a beat.

19

TEJANO MUSIC IS BLARING OUT OF THE SPEAKERS in Juerez's Bodega a few blocks from my house. I search the store for chocolate sauce and the potato chips that Laura loves. Little kids run up and down the aisles and are being yelled at in Spanish by the man at the counter.

I find Laura's chips and turn the corner to get the chocolate sauce and run smack into Jason. Three little kids squeeze past us with juice boxes in their hands and run to the back of the store.

Jason watches them go—smiling.

"They got some serious sugar on."

"Yeah, I guess so," I say.

The bodega's aisle isn't that wide, and Jason takes up a lot of it.

We stand looking at the floor for a few seconds.

Jason says, "How you been? I don't think I've talked to you since the accident." He looks at the brace on my knee. Most times I try to pretend like I'm just sporting a knee pad. Misha talks to me about being in denial.

"I'm okay," I say.

"Good," he says. Then I notice he's got a couple of six packs under his arm.

"Party?"

"Yeah—small party," he says.

All I can think about and not say is Jason's having a bad year. One of his friends is dead and the girl he's really starting to like (I think) is hooking up with a security guard/musician with a bad comic-book habit. And worse—he's trying to be nice to the person responsible for killing his friend.

Okay—I don't say that to anybody. I don't ever want to say it out loud. But I know. I really know. Kris would have been home safe if I hadn't been on the train. He would still be on the school paper. He'd still be kickin' it with his boys. He'd still . . . be, if not for me.

My knee starts to hurt and I must look like I'm in real pain 'cause Jason says, "Can I give you a ride home? You aren't making me go out of my way, remember. I live real close to you."

At first I think no, just because. Then I change my mind 'cause those blocks are looking longer as my knee is starting to howl. So I nod, find my chocolate sauce, and head up to the counter behind Jason.

Jason flashes an ID and the man puts each six in a plastic bag after Jason hands over the cash. I go to pay for the chips and sauce but Jason puts the money down. When I slide the bills back over to him he moves out the door without taking it. The man at the counter shrugs and takes the money. I head out the door behind Jason. Now even on the busy street everything seems quieter. I didn't get just how loud the music was in the store.

"Where'd you get the fake ID?"

Jason points across the street to where his car is. It's way busy now. Jason takes me by the arm he's holding the beer under, then puts the other arm out to signal for the oncoming, crazy-assed, after-work traffic to stop. And it's wild when it does. We get across the street in one piece. I look at Jason like he's some kind of magician.

When he clicks the remote I open the

passenger-side door and raise myself up into the SUV. He puts the beer in the back, then climbs in.

He turns and smiles at me. "It's my brother's ID. He thinks he lost it so he had to get another one. I only use this sometimes."

"Ummmmmm?"

"No, really." Then he starts to laugh as he pulls out into traffic.

Jason puts in a CD and says, "You want to go to Metroparks or do you need to get back right now?"

"Naw, I don't have to get back right away. I'll call home." But first I put the money for the chips and chocolate in his jacket pocket. He smiles.

I get my cell out of my pocket and call Laura to tell her I'll be home before dinner and that I got her chips. She's okay with it. At least she's trying to be okay with letting me out of the house at all. I can tell by the way she watches me anytime I leave that she wants to lock me in my room. It's worse when she's been at the hospital visiting Keone all day.

We drive through the traffic on Euclid Ave.—which is like a zoo—for about ten minutes talking about nothing. Then we're in the 'burbs. In two turns we're getting out of the car and heading into the park. We walk—Jason keeps supporting me with his arm—and even though we're walking real slow I stumble over branches, leaves, and assorted holes. Funny, until today I was more sure-footed even with the knee brace on. What the hell is wrong with me?

Jason smells so good. No, wait. What? I'm just finding this out? Where the hell have I been? Who the hell is he anyway? Ummmm, he still smells so good . . .

We walk for a couple of minutes in the cool breeze, inhaling wood smoke. Up ahead we find a picnic table sitting right beside the creek. Jason pulls a bottle of beer out of his jacket pocket, twists off the top, throws it in the garbage can by the table, and drinks half the bottle in one swallow.

Impressive.

He offers me the rest, but I shake my head. I'm not really into beer drinking. It's too bitter. But I do jack drinks when Laura's sisters come over for Midnight Margaritas once a month and they aren't looking.

Jason says, "Good for you," and drinks the rest while he looks off into the trees.

I watch the creek as it flows by us, carrying leaves and the occasional branch. A few minutes later two little boys and a dog go running by, screaming and laughing. The dog sees us, stops, and flops on her back. We get off the table and scratch her stomach. She lies there in dog heaven for a couple of minutes until the little boys call her. Then she's gone and I'm sitting on the ground next to Jason.

. . . and he still smells so good.

. . . and it doesn't matter that much that his mouth tastes a little like beer as we start to kiss. Jason stands and steers me towards a mammoth oak tree and soon we're against it and he's pulling my T-shirt up and I've pulled his jacket off and have slipped my hands underneath his shirt. His chest is smooth and warm. And he probably thinks the same thing about mine, 'cause there's not much there, sadly.

And this must be what it's like when something feels so good you don't want to stop. I don't want to, ever, so I start to unzip his jeans and he lets me. But just as he starts to unzip mine and has gotten halfway—he stops.

"I don't have anything, Scotty."

"What?" I say like I'm coming out of a dream.

"I got no protection. No rubbers. Are you on the pill?"

"The pill?" I swear I draw a blank.

"Yeah—the pill."

I inhale and lean against Jason, who I realize is almost a foot taller than me. He's been leaning against the tree on a slide all this time to try to be eye to eye with me. He kisses me again and his tongue is warm and slow in my mouth. I don't taste the beer anymore.

Then he kisses me between my breasts but stops when I inhale.

"Are you, Scotty, on the pill?"

"No."

He kisses me again, then slowly zips my pants up and pulls down my T-shirt and bra. He exhales and zips his own jeans back up, then pulls me to him, again.

"Girl, you feel too damned good."

"So do you," I say.

Jason pulls his shirt down and reaches to get his jacket. He zips it up and holds me tight. I feel him all over and breathe him in. He smells like fall, spices and soap. Then he takes me by the arm and gently leads me back to the car. When he pulls into my driveway he gets out and opens my door for me (like my dad does for Laura) while I scoop up the bag of chips and choco-late sauce. Then he walks me to my front door, kisses me again, and stands there till I go in.

When I wake up around two in the morning the only reason I know it wasn't a dream is that I still smell like him.

Then I think—oh hell.

PART 5

Folks

20

YESTERDAY FALCONE GOT A PHONE CALL BACK FROM his sister Gina. She said, "It's not a good time to come visit me. But I miss you. Tell me how you and Misha and Scotty are. Is there something that you need? Any of you? I *miss* you all and it sometimes seems you are all a dream as you get older and I see you less. If you don't need anything, tell me everything . . ."

They talked for an hour. He said they talked about everything and nothing at all.

Yesterday I got on a bus, got dropped off in Kris's neighborhood, and stood across the street until his mother came out to get the mail. She looked at me, then at the brace on my knee, squinted at me some more, then went quietly back into the house without getting her mail.

Yesterday Misha finally read a letter from her parents that she'd had for over a month (her father thinks e-mail is destroying the whole world's ability to write letters) that they were going to spend another semester in South Africa and might go to Ghana after that. They'd promised Misha that by her sophomore year they'd be stable and at home. Misha wouldn't have to live with the Aunts. We are all juniors now.

She holds on to the letters a while so she can defend herself from the hurt that usually comes.

I went home and burned Misha a mix CD. Then I put it, three candy bars, and two postcards of Mexico with a picture I took of Nougat Boy on my phone when he wasn't watching, wrapped that baby up with Misha's address on it, and asked Laura to post it for me before she went to the hospital.

When Laura left I began to read some more *Anna Karenina*. I think when it was written it was just a dramatic love story that became more important to people with the passage of time. Who knows? I got the mail out of the slot and walked through the house listening to the quiet. Laura finally came back home and is in her office. She looked up at me. An hour later I am still curled up beside her on the couch. Just me, her, and her laptop.

"I mailed your package to Misha."

"It's not from me—it's from Nougat Boy. They need to love each other and be together."

Laura sighs and says, "Oh."

Laura has never acted like she loves Keone any better than me because he's her biological child. But sometimes other people say things. Like we'll be in the mall and someone who is only just acquainted with the family will come up and say, "You look too good to have a child her age." Then something like, "Oh yeah, I forgot; you aren't her real mother."

That's when Laura smiles real sweet and says—deadly—"If I'm not her real mother I don't know who the hell is." Then she takes me by the hand and walks off. I'd feel sorry for these people if they weren't so stupid. They don't know Laura.

I do.

You never know about folks.

21

I REFRESH THE BAG OF GINGERSNAPS BESIDE KEONE'S bed. We tell all the nurses and aides to eat them if they want. I like the idea of Keone hearing cookies munching. That has to be his favorite sound in the world. Maybe it will wake him up.

Then I make sure his plane, train, and automobile books are always within arm's reach in case he wakes up. Laura is straightening his room and just brought him another comforter, this one with cars on it. She fluffs the comforter, then pulls up a chair and starts reading a novel.

I sit beside her and she puts down her book.

"I've been thinking of you, Scotty."

She takes my hands gently and rubs them when she feels the cold.

"I'm around."

"I see that, but I'm not seeing very much of you."

"I try to see the boy when you aren't here so he won't have so much alone time."

She says, "I know. How is your knee? Your leg? Your body?"

"Better."

"And your heart?"

I want to say broken, bruised, confused, guilty, and cold. But all I end up doing is faking a smile, then breaking down and crying—again like a baby. Laura lets me blubber on her until I look up and see the streetlights starting to shine through Keone's hospital window. He hasn't moved, and life is going on. I want to tell her about stupid stuff that used to be fun to talk about before her baby ended up in a coma.

I forget it all and keep on crying.

I haven't told anybody about me and Jason in the park, because I don't know what that was about. It's not like I cheated on a friend, 'cause Misha isn't into him—she's got Thelonious on the brain—so I guess I can tell her later. I don't know what it is. I can't sit down again. I feel like there's something I'm supposed to do. Then I remember, so I dash into the girls' bathroom and hide in a stall, pull out my phone, and make a call to a bakery.

I think of Falcone—he won't give anybody advice about stuff like this, 'cause it's only been three months since he broke up with Nick. And that was ugly, since all of us—including Falcone's papi—loved Nick. We couldn't help ourselves. We'd invite him to things after the breakup. Falcone was almost ready to break up with us. I think it's time for him to get over it and go back with Nick . . . with just a little help from a friend.

That makes me think about Jason even more. And it makes me think everybody is wrong about love and sex and heartache. I don't think there should be guilt. I never even looked at or thought about him that way before that day in the park. It just happened. So I think it was just about the loneliness and anguish of us both losing a boy I was just about to know.

Nothing is making it go away.

But in school Jason stares at me across the lunchroom. In the hallway he leans against his locker and watches me walk down the hall.

"Scotts. Scotty?"

His voice is like candy. Like caramel. I limp away as fast as I can and act like I haven't heard him, which is easy to do when classes let out and everyone is talking like everybody else is deaf.

"Scotty."

Again with the Scotty. Doesn't he know he's going to make me pull out all my hair . . . or run at him and kiss him till his lips hurt? Either one won't look good during class break. I dart in front of Darryl Willis and Kyle Gallagher—who are probably twenty feet wide together. They are the line on the football team. I lose him.

When we pass on the stairs later that day he walks just close enough to brush against my arm. And when he tries to talk to me I almost fall down the stairs 'cause a freshman with a giant papier-mâché clown gets between us. He catches me before I tumble down the stairs like my mom's old Slinky.

I gurgle—"Thanks"—and run. Ummmm, limp quickly.

Is it wrong that I just want to kiss him all over the face in front of the bio lab, where it's obvious someone has had an accident with sulfur?

I feel embarrassed, and I probably made him feel stupid.

No way can I be in a limo with him in a couple of days.

How am I supposed to tell the difference

between sex and love since I've technically only had something that wasn't really sex and I don't think I've ever been in love . . . maybe? Unless the stomachache and sweaty palms I have are Ebola.

TODAY I FOUND MY DAD OUTSIDE THE SHED OILING everything in sight.

He watched me climb over some lawn chairs, a ladder, and an old scarecrow we used to put in the front yard until Laura caught Keone hiding cookies in it. Crazy, but true.

"What up, parent?"

"Just doing what I should have done a few weeks ago."

I say, "Want some help?"

He looks at me, laughs, and shakes his head. He knows all I'll do is get in the way and eventually start whining.

"How about you just be some company, Scotts—no help?"

Fine by me.

I know it's going to be enough just to sit next to him.

"Did you know that when I went into Keone's room to take some more train books to him I found a photo album?"

"Nope," I say.

Dad shakes the last oil out of a can and opens a new one.

"I thought Laura might have told you about it."

"She's been busy, Dad. With the hospital and all. Work. You know."

He smiles.

I start to scoop up leaves that have fallen from our backyard maple tree and begin to cover my legs, then my thighs, and finally my torso with them. It's always what I love best about fall. I can only get Keone to let me cover him in leaves if I bribe him with something sweet, round, and crunchy.

So for the next hour, I become leaf girl and my dad oils anything that's metal and glances at me when he doesn't think I'm looking. I feel like a little kid again and it feels just fine.

Dad pulls up one of the plastic lawn chairs and watches some leaves tumble to the ground and says, "Keone keeps a photo album."

I sit up and stare at my dad after having cov-ered my whole body with the sweetish-smelling leaves.

"There are pages and pages of trains he's cut out from the train magazines I buy him. And on each train there is a photo he has glued of some-one he knows in front of the engine. Their faces are completely round, and he always makes sure they are attached to the same train, over and over. You know—just like my head belongs to my body."

I stare at my dad.

I like him a lot. Always have, especially when he seems puzzled—like now.

"Are you saying Keone sees us all as certain trains?"

Dad nods and his eyes look sad.

He leaves his chair and goes back to oiling and cleaning tools that will be put away for the winter.

I guess I never really thought how hard hav-ing an autistic son was on my father. He never seemed upset about it and has the patience of ten people. I mean, sometimes I do wonder what a world with a "normal" Keone would look like.

But Dad blows me away by saying—"I

wonder what he was thinking when his beloved train crashed as he was riding it to get home?"

I lie on my side and watch more leaves fall to the ground. I am too tired to cover myself up anymore.

23

THERE'S TOO MUCH FOOD AT MISHA'S HOUSE JUST
to be feeding Thelonious. You'd think they had
about twenty people living there instead of just
Misha and her five skinny aunts.

Thelonious sits beside Misha eating tons of
spaghetti and meatballs, baskets of garlic bread,
and about a bushel of salad. The Aunts love
him. They love anyone who can throw down
on some food. Misha told me they loved Jason
too—the one time he came over.

The Aunts will feed anybody. They also think
anybody going to a dance with their niece—who
is costing them serious coin on a dress, shoes,
hair, and nails, plus her part in the limo—should
at least show up and let them check him out and
maybe run a background check (Jacks's thing).

With Jason they got all-American scholar, athlete, hot dude.

With Thelonious they get artistic, geek, *X-Men*-loving musician.

They seem to love Thelonious and so does Misha.

Falcone sits next to me stuffing his face (we decided to come for dessert) and isn't adding to the conversation. Which is why he was invited in the first place. No worries, though, 'cause Thelonious can hold his own.

The Aunts—Lynn, Adrienne, Caroline, Costella, and Jacks—laugh and talk about everything at dinner. Lynn says to Thelonious, "Misha says you lived in Mexico for a long time."

Thelonious nods, swallows, and says, "Yeah, I lived in Mexico City with my dad. He traveled a lot. After that I came back to the States to live with my mom up in the mountains."

"What mountains?" I ask.

"Blue Ridge. I lived in North Carolina for a few years with her. She's a weaver," he says.

"It must have been beautiful in the mountains," I say.

Thelonious gives Misha a crooked grin. He grabs her hand, looks into her eyes, and says, "It's pretty beautiful around here, too."

Falcone coughs.

The Aunts sigh and/or giggle.

Then the conversation veers off about cars and soup. I don't know what thread they used to link the two. I just look at Misha grinning like an idiot. She's so happy. Falcone is happy because his mouth has food in it. Thelonious is happy because of Misha and the food. The Aunts are happy 'cause everybody is eating their food.

I just sit here chewing on garlic bread and thinking about love and the look on Nick's face the other day when that clown delivered his basket of cookies to the school. He looked freaked when the clown walked towards him near the gym while everybody laughed. Then he looked damned relieved when the clown left the cookies and walked away. I pretended not to notice when Nick read the card attached to the basket of peanut butter cookies and slowly started to smile.

PART 6

Autumn

24

FALCONE STANDS BEHIND ME AS I PUT EACH individual flower on the grave. He's whispering something, or maybe he's singing. Whatever he's doing I don't mind it. This is the second time in two weeks that Falcone has brought me here. After all the flowers are gone I sit down on the ground next to Kris's grave.

He keeps whispering.

I missed Kris's funeral. Laura lay beside me on my bed that afternoon while I cried until my eyes shut from swelling. Kris's mom didn't want me there. She couldn't help herself. She knew the truth that nobody else would talk about. She knew the way it all happened but wasn't supposed to. Kris's mom knew it was all my fault that he wouldn't ever come home, graduate, go to college, get a job, get married, and have babies and grandbabies.

I stole it all from him and her.

And I think about him every day, after years of only thinking about him as the boy who put gum in my hair and forced me to be bald. I went years not even talking to him. I should have kept doing that. I should have kept being pissed and snarky whenever he was around.

Now I can't go five minutes anymore not thinking about Kris. I'll be laughing or reading—then *slam*, his face, his eyes, his voice will come out of nowhere. I remember his laugh just as the train started braking. I remember his hand pulling me back and the other one reaching out for Keone as he flew through the air.

Falcone takes my hand and we start to walk back to the car.

I read tombstones as we walk.

I say, "They always say the nicest things about you when you're gone."

Falcone squeezes my hand and says, "Yeah, it's all about what everybody should have said. I think I'll have them put 'never mind' on my headstone."

"I like that," I say.

We let go of hands as we split to go past a tree—then grab hands again when we clear it. As we walk past the headstones and monuments I think how cemeteries end up being about the living, and how they want to remember the dead. I think if the dead had their say there'd be a whole lot more parties going on in here. And I don't know why, but that makes me cry.

Falcone puts his arm around me and doesn't say anything. What can he say? What can I tell him? It's hard to talk about a dead boy that you only held a single conversation longer than thirty seconds with since you were nine. Then you sit beside him, he laughs, you think he's more than okay, and you can even see through to forgiving him for making you bald. Then he's gone and everybody around you knows more about him than you.

Falcone starts whispering again.

I lean closer to him and brush the hair away from his face.

"What are you saying?"

Falcone looks at me, surprised.

"I'm praying."

"Praying?"

"Yeah, praying. Weren't you praying by the grave?"

"I don't think I've ever prayed. My mom used to take me to Sunday school, but I only remember that she gave me peppermint gum and I always fell asleep."

Falcone nods and holds me tighter when a cold breeze makes us both shiver.

"Gina used to take me to church. My dad— not so much."

"I never went after my mom died. I don't think my dad believes."

We get to the car and instead of getting in sit on the hood.

"You don't think he believes in what? Praying or God?

"I don't know," I say.

"What do you believe in, Scotty?"

"I don't know."

I lean closer to Falcone and try not to start crying again, but the tears roll down my face. Falcone offer his sleeve as we sit and watch the rest of the leaves find their way down.

Falcone wipes away some more of my tears.

"Never mind," he says.

25

I SHOULDN'T HAVE EATEN THAT SECOND PIECE OF pecan pie. The Endangered Species could make a pie to make you cry. I knew it was tofu day at home and that Laura had said it would be Thai today. I don't want Laura to think I'm an ingrate and don't appreciate what she cooks—even when I don't.

But the pie was good and the crowd was happening. A couple of artists from the loft across the street were eating steak and eggs. They hardly ever come out in the daylight. A delivery man was swigging coffee and yelling at somebody on his cell that his GPS wasn't work-ing, and a woman with three kids was trying to get her set of twins to share an order of fries—and failing.

School let out twenty minutes ago and there was no place I needed to be so here was good.

I'm just about to pick up a pecan that's fallen off my second piece of pie when Jason sits down next to me. He's there so fast I can't even embarrass myself by sliding under the table and/ or making a run for it.

"Okay, Scotty, we're in a real small diner and there's no place you can sprint off to, duck under, or hide behind."

Again, it would help me out more if Jason didn't always smell so damned good.

I lie. "I haven't been running from you."

"Scotty."

"I haven't."

"Scotty."

Jason relaxes, 'cause I guess he realizes I'm going to keep denying it. That way I don't have to be as ashamed as I really am. But I'll be damned if he doesn't read my mind.

"Scotty, I'm sorry about the park. I mean— I'm not sorry it happened. I just mean I'm sorry that I took advantage. I feel like you might think I wasn't respecting you the way I came at you. I mean—"

"Okay, stop." I need another piece of pie— but there's still tofu for dinner.

Jason closes his eyes and doesn't say anything else for the minute. I pretend I'm eating whatever is left on the dessert plate in front of me. My favorite green-haired waitress comes over and smiles at Jason.

"What'll you have, darling?"

He opens his eyes and points at my plate. "I'll have what she had."

I stop imaginary pie eating and relax back against the booth. Now two men in suits and a woman dressed for a formal walk in. She leans over the counter and the green-haired waitress gives her a carryout bag. Ms. Sparkly Formal pays and is out the door in front of the lost delivery man.

Jason gets his pie in a minute, the waitress calls him darling again, then he moves closer to me and says, "Share?"

And that's how we sit at the Endangered Species, smiling and eating pie.

I call Falcone's house but his dad says he went for a drive with somebody. Me being nosy, I ask, "Who?" He says Falcone grumbled a name he couldn't hear, kept looking in the mirror and messing with his hair, then finally left with a big old dumb smile on his face.

Later that night I start to smile again when I think of the clown walking towards Nick and how my hand is still warm from holding Jason's before I fall asleep.

26

I GOT MY HOMECOMING DRESS TODAY FROM Celia's Closet. Celia is a friend of Laura's. The dress found me in her little shop off of Coventry. Celia is a witch's granddaughter. I figured I'd waited so long to get a dress, the only way I was ever going to get one was to stop looking for it. So just as I was reaching for an old picture book from the forties about trains, I spotted it from across the room.

I'm getting excited that homecoming falls on Halloween. Definitely more choices of dresses to wear when people are walking around as zombies and dead accountants and vampires. Celia's Closet is full of everything. And I mean everything. It's worth the forty-minute bus ride just to touch and smell the things in the store. Some things in the shop are on consignment, but not everything. But when I walk over to a flowing green dress—it acts like it found me and won't let go.

Celia claps her hands when I walk out of the dressing room.

"No one has been able to fit into that dress—until you."

I out-twirl Misha and cannot believe the fit. It's a beautiful gauzy sage green that fits like it was made for me. It's sleeveless and has a very slight train in the back that brushes the floor, barely.

"People were a lot smaller way back then," Celia says.

"This dress is that old?" I say.

"Do you care?" Celia asks, in her black head wrap and gold caftan.

"No, I don't."

Then she says, "I have a necklace that belonged to a witch—one of my grandmother's friends, actually."

"Was she a good witch or a bad witch?"

Celia walks off to find me the necklace to go with the dress.

She brings back a beautiful teardrop crystal necklace and latches it around my neck.

"She was an amazingly *good* witch. She changed people's lives for the *good* without them ever knowing it."

So when I leave out of Celia's with my sage green dress and the amazingly good witch's necklace, I also relieve her of an extremely old copy of *The Railroad's Western Journey* for Keone.

The halls are quiet in pediatrics. I open Keone's door and the room smells like ginger. His books are stacked waiting for him and the music he loves plays just low enough for him and not too loud that anyone outside his room could hear. They say he might actually hear everything going on around him, even though he's still in a coma. I like to believe that.

I take the book out I bought from Celia's, then put it on top of the four or five books already beside his bed. It's got that old book smell Keone likes.

"Keone, do you want me to try on my witch dress for you?"

Keone never likes to try on clothes himself but he always loves to watch other people walk back and forth in front of a mirror at the mall. I think he sees it as a game, maybe. He loves it. I go into his bathroom and put the dress on. There's a full-length mirror on the back of the bathroom door and even in the bad lighting it's still beautiful. I open the door and walk towards Keone. You can't tell that he's been asleep for weeks.

The Band-Aids are coming off slowly.

No more wrapped left hand. Then the bandage on the right arm came off. The swelling in his face went down; then the head wrap came off. Every day Keone looks more like Keone.

So I stand beside my little brother's bed in my green witch dress and begin to twirl around his room. I dance to the music coming out of the boom box from the jazz channel. I dance around the room and read out loud to Keone about trains, cars, planes and anything that moves, rolls, or flies.

I'm tired at the end of the twirling so I climb into bed with Keone and read him his favorite book about trains. I fall asleep holding my little brother's hand.

I walk out of pediatrics with the witch dress in my bag again and the crystal necklace sliding around in the bottom. The train book from Celia's I leave tucked beside Keone underneath his comforter. When I walk out of his room I feel the jazz music following me home—little bitty ghosts of my sleeping brother.

As I get on the bus and find a seat towards the middle I look up towards his room and smile. At least I showed him my homecoming dress.

And I start to think about evil omens. It's one of the things that's stayed with me from *Anna Karenina*. Trains and omens. And of course I haven't finished the book report yet. I think I will take the incomplete at this point.

But at that moment I would have hollered and kissed everybody on the bus if I'd known that Keone was waking up just as I sat down beside the snoring kid with the backpack on the Cain Park/East Cleveland bus. By the time I got home—though I still didn't know it—he was totally awake and wrapping his arms around *The Railroad's Western Journey* and was probably wondering if I would maybe come back soon and dance again in the green witch dress.

I always miss the best stories in the making.

The nurse told us all she knew about Keone waking up.

One minute a nurse at the station thought she saw a little kid darting behind the desk. Then he was gone. Another nurse thought she heard someone eating something crunchy over by the fridge where they keep juice and ginger ale for the kids. Another nurse finally went in Keone's room, where he had a bunch of cookies in the middle of the floor, a ginger ale, a stethoscope, and a pile of train books surrounding him. And because he knew he was truly a superhero, Keone was naked and using his hospital gown as a cape.

I wished I'd gone and seen him an hour later than I did.

My brother is Superman.

27

Hurray for Halloween
Hurray for Halloween
Owls hoot
whoooooo
And cats meow
meeoowww
And witches fly up in the sky
Hurray
for
Hal-lo-ween
Boo!

I say, "Now let's all thank Misha for that talent-filled rendition of an amazing Halloween song I think she made up."

Misha is hanging out the moon top of the parked limo, rockin' a huge turban around her head.

"I DIDN'T MAKE IT UP," she yells. I guess you gotta scream if you're hanging out the moon top of a limo. Her aunt Adrienne tries to wave her down.

When it doesn't work she says, "Misha, get down from there. Can you pretend to be a grown-up for about five minutes?"

"No—I mean yeah," she says, getting out of the car and taking her jeweled sandals off. Her mask is tied to her wrist. We all have them.

It seems like half the neighborhood is out standing in yards snapping pictures of kids in formal dresses and tuxes. But there's Misha back up in the moon roof of one of the biggest truck-looking limos I've ever seen. I'm kind of embarrassed at having the big-assed thing in front of the house.

I wrap my arms around Misha and we grin like idiots for my dad as he takes picture after picture.

"More poses, girls."

Mr. Alguero pulls up in a few seconds. Falcone looks like a model in his tux. He walks over and squeezes between us. We hug him and start playing to the camera again. The more people, the more poses. And I start to think how just an hour ago we were all somewhere else that didn't have us in high heels, long dresses, and updos.

Falcone touches my hair softly and stares at Misha's.

"Who did your hair, Scotty?"

I say, "Michelle did mine."

She had half of Heights High battling for seats in her shop. When the electricity flashed for five seconds I thought half the girls would have to get CPR. Anyway, Michelle's did seriously good. I know a lot of people who end up with helmet hair when they go to get updos.

Okay—Misha is wearing the amazing backless black lace dress that doesn't hang down to the ground as much as it drifts like snow. She's wearing a thin silver necklace with baby teardrops hanging from it. Her shoes (she's holding in her hands) are jeweled satin—black and turquoise.

Laura and Mr. Alguero have been looking at her like they are expecting something to emerge from Misha's turban. Falcone just says, "Shopping with the Mad Hatter?"

And all she says is . . . "It matches."

I say, "Misha, why are you hiding your locks?"

Misha grabs Falcone and me for more pictures and totally blows the question off. I can't believe she's hiding her locks. Did Mrs. Williams ask her to? 'Cause if she did she needs some cultural sensitivity classes. If not, Misha is deluded that the head wrap looks good on her. And I'm just about to pull her over to the side of the maple tree and say so when another car pulls up behind the limo. The limo driver has been leaning against the car in dark glasses taking everything in and answering questions my dad's been throwing at him between pictures.

Falcone announces that the next two minutes of photos will be just of him so that he can send them to his sister, Gina. Flashes everywhere.

The car door opens and Jason walks out. Another door opens and Nick gets out. The last door opens and Thelonious is standing there. Falcone smiles and whispers something under his breath. . . . Misha and I stand there. Her mouth is open in shock and I have a shit-eatin' grin on mine.

Thelonious goes up to turban girl—I mean Misha.

Nick goes over to Falcone, who once upon

a time never wanted to see him again but now wraps his arms around him like they've never been apart.

And Jason walks over to me.

My dad, Misha's aunt Adrienne, and Mr. Alguero go crazy with the cameras. Laura runs around hugging everybody. She's been hugging anybody who stands still long enough ever since Keone woke up, nakedly terrorizing pediatrics.

It's almost perfect. We head to Jason's house so his, Nick's, and Thelonious's people can ooh and aah us. And then we all finally climb back into the limo laughing and waving and pouring Cokes into crystal glasses and we toast Halloween as the limo blows down the leaf-covered road.

And about the time we are blocks from the school, Kris's mother is opening a red box with a framed photo of her beautiful son laughing when he was about nine years old. What has been cropped out of the photo is the little girl with the gum in her hair, frowning.

28

I DON'T GO TO FOOTBALL GAMES—WELL, I DON'T
go to many of them. But I always like the way
the lights glow blocks away when the football
field is lit up. I don't know why, but they have
the lights on the field lit tonight. The dance is
in the gym, though. The homecoming queen
used to be picked at the football game the night
before the dance. I guess there were some bad
scenes where the visitors' fans booed and got
out of hand. Nobody wanted the homecoming
queen booed. So—they pick her at the dance
now.

The theme is "A Halloween Homecoming,"
which wasn't so easy to keep as the theme 'cause
two churches picketed the school when they

found out and a couple of parents (from the two churches) even threatened to take their kids out of school. They carried signs that said KEEP DEVIL WORSHIPERS OUT OF HOMECOMING. Damn. It's still the Midwest around here, no matter how many open-minded people you surround yourself with.

Everyone is supposed to wear a mask as the dance is a masked ball. Mine has feathers and kitty whiskers. I love the way everybody who's usually dressed in jeans now is dressed in mad crazy dresses and tuxes and nobody knows who anybody else is. We all climb out of the limo and line up for more pictures before we go into the gym. Again there are so many cameras flashing and people all around that I lose Misha.

Jason stays right beside me, though.

"You okay?"

"Yeah, but I've lost Misha."

"I think I saw her go in."

I jump straight up trying to get a view over everybody to see if I can find her.

"There's Thelonious, Falcone, and Nick standing near the fountain."

Nick and Thelonious have taken their masks off and are laughing about something. Falcone's shaking his head, then spots me jumping up and down and pushes his way through the crowd still getting their pictures taken outside the gym.

Falcone is still holding his mask when he grabs my hand.

"Yo, Jason, can I borrow your girl a minute?"

Jason leans close, lifts my mask and kisses me, and says, "Yeah, for a minute."

(Okay, pause . . . I do believe that was our very first official kiss. Since I pretty much blocked out much of what happened at the park—except the parts that make my eyes go huge—I technically don't count the lip-locking in the woods as a first kiss.)

Stop pause. I almost passed out from this kiss.

Falcone holds me up as I walk away with him, looking back at Jason.

"Okayyy, what's up that I had to walk away from the cute boy?"

"What's your girl up to with the head wear, Scotty?"

"Who?"

"Who? Misha, Scotty, Misha. What's she up to?"

I guess I look clueless, 'cause he leads me back to Jason, then we all walk into the gym as the line thins. Just inside the door on a table with a burgundy tablecloth there's a poster-sized framed photo of Kris, with a lot of people standing around it. Some cry; some just touch the flowers around the table.

And like all the times before, when I show up, everybody divides, looks at me like I'm the most pitiful thing on the planet, then moves away. So in the end I'm standing alone at the table. And there's Kris—smiling and not knowing that his picture would be the only way he'd get to come be with everybody at the dance this year.

29

THE GYM IS DECORATED WITH GLOWING jack-o'-lanterns, silvery ghosts that hang from the ceiling, and something that looks like spiderwebs draped across the rafters and almost anywhere people lean or sit. The individual tables have candles in the shapes of bats, and the music is loud.

I spend most of the night nodding my head and not really understanding much of what anybody says to me.

I dance with Jason.

Then Nick.

Then Falcone.

Then with Thelonious.

Then with DJ Hampton, who used to chase

me home, trying to put fake spiders on me, and was a good friend to Kris. I figure tonight would be appropriate for him to chase me around the room with one of them, but he doesn't. He just dances with me and his date, and screams in our ears like everybody else does. I don't think he cares if I hear what he says.

Misha dances with Thelonious most of the night. That girl's in love.

I go to our table to take my shoes off for a minute and pick at the food that I got at the buffet. The DJ keeps on hittin' everybody with music they can't help but dance to.

I drink some punch and think about taking a few of the pumpkin cookies to Keone in the hospital. I watch as Misha finally dances with her original date, Jason. It makes me smile. In a minute Falcone is sitting next to me with a plate packed with buffalo wings.

We scream at each other over the music, eat, and finally get a break when a slow song fills the gym.

"How's Nick?"

Falcone smiles between bites.

"He's fine. Damn—who'da thunk it? Did I tell you Nick thinks it's been me sending him things in the mail and sending clowns over to

him with cookies? And you were too busy trying to drink up all the soda in the limo to try to
get any info out of him for me. I've just been
going along with it—as has Misha. Misha was
too busy having that big-assed turban on her
head and insisting we all listen to some mix
CD Thelonious made for her. Jason was just
too cool and calm to think any of it was crazy. I
mean—right?"

"Ummmhuh," I say.

Then, "So did you know about me and
Jason?"

"No. And we'll talk about that later."

"What about you and Nick? How's that
working out?"

Falcone hisses in my ear, "We'll talk about
that later too, dear Ms. Cookie Clown Monster."

Luckily Falcone swallows the last of the wings
just as the song is over and the homecoming
committee chair Maya Jacobs takes the stage in
front of the DJ in a long black dress. She thanks
everybody on the committee and everyone who
had anything to do with the decorations, selling
tickets, the food, the setup, the photographers,
and security and the junior class for the photo of
Kris. Then she starts thanking the faculty.

Jason, Nick, and Thelonious wander over

to the table we're sharing with DJ and a girl named Rae who doesn't go to our school. In a minute all the homecoming court will line the stage, starting with the freshman, sophomore, and junior attendants. Misha with her junior ass went missing a while ago to get ready. She waved to me as she headed towards the hallway.

I'm starting to get butterflies. As much as Misha fights it, I'm glad she was chosen for the court as the junior attendant. I think she could be the queen next year 'cause she's in-your-face, smart, understanding, independent. So I hold my breath as the room starts to get a little tense. It's a miracle Misha wasn't asked to step down from the court because she and Mrs. Williams never could get along. Even up to a few days ago the woman was trying to get Misha to cover up her tat. I thought Misha would bounce a long time ago. Anyway the junior attendant crowns the senior queen. So where was Misha?

So what happened next shouldn't have been a surprise.

I mean it was—but it shouldn't have been.

When Maya Jacobs finally stops thanking the street light for changing and letting everybody get here safely tonight, the homecoming court walks onto the stage from the wings.

Freshman attendant Jameela Hopkins, kind and generous (lends me lunch money).

Sophomore attendant Deborah Holmes (volunteers at a homeless shelter).

Junior attendant Misha Northrup (friend, feminist, and . . . Bride of Frankenstein).

The whole gym goes crazy. Everybody is laughing so hard and jumping in front of people with cameras and phones that I have to climb up on my chair with my banged-up knee to see her. The stupid turban was hiding a fright wig and now Misha is wearing a hospital gown and men's Timberlands without socks. It looks like she's put some grayish paint on her face as she waves to the crowd like a zombie. The whole gym is in hysterics as the Bride keeps waving with big scary eyes and no smile.

I catch a look at Mrs. Williams on the side of the stage where a minute ago she was directing the court. She looks like she might be having a seizure just as the Bride breaks out of the line, walks over to her, points, and opens her mouth in a silent scream.

And oh yeah, Nori Morris (takes everybody's boyfriend and is proud of it—voted in by the football, baseball, and boys' track teams) won homecoming queen.

And that was the homecoming dance.

It's the last day in October.

The rain held off the whole night and I was so happy about that. Wet formal wear isn't what anybody had in mind. At the end of the night we all climb back into the limo—which is stocked with carbonated stuff again.

Misha's head is on my shoulder and I'm trying not to pee myself as she tells me how she freaked the court out when she pulled off her turban in the locker room. Jason, Nick, Thelonious, and Falcone haven't stopped laughing between drinks of who-knows-what they've got in plastic cups. They'll need the facilities soon too.

The limo driver takes us the long way home through downtown. Everything is quiet and the streets are almost empty as it's one o'clock on Sunday morning. He leaves downtown Cleveland and heads for the Shoreway as we look out onto a cold dark Lake Erie—then drives us all back home to East Cleveland and I'm happier than I thought I would ever be again.

And maybe life just doesn't happen. Maybe

it is a story, always changing, never giving you the ending it seems to be working up to. I'm not feeling as bruised and tragic as I have been feeling, with all my friends around me now. I don't think some of the sadness is something I'll think about later this morning when the rain is beating down on my bedroom window and making me feel like it's softly raining all over the world.

ABOUT THE AUTHOR

Angela Johnson has won three Coretta Scott King Awards, one each for her novels *Heaven*, *Toning the Sweep*, and *The First Part Last*. Her latest novel, *Sweet, Hereafter*, completed the Heaven trilogy. In recognition of her outstanding talent, Angela was named a 2003 MacArthur Fellow. She lives in Kent, Ohio.